SMASHIE McPERTER
AND THE
MYSTERY OF
THE MISSING GOOP

NPL | **F**
Nashville Public Library | FOUNDATION

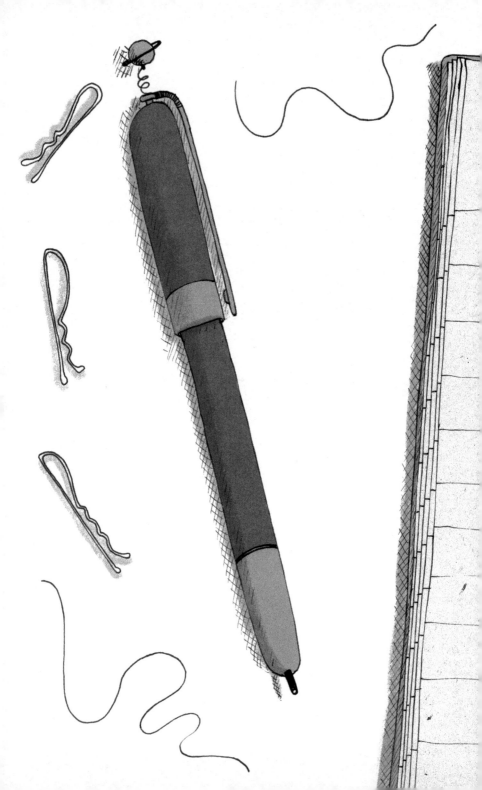

SMASHIE McPERTER
AND THE MYSTERY OF THE MISSING GOOP

N. GRIFFIN

illustrated by
KATE HINDLEY

CANDLEWICK PRESS

So many lovely people helped this book become a book! I'd like to thank
Tobin, Jane, Allen, Ann, and Susan for their eagle-like reading eyes.
Big thanks to Kristin for helping with the dance research, and HUGE thanks
to Esme for helping me with the secret messages. I'd also like to thank my
wonderful agent, Linda Pratt, and my super-duper editor, Karen Lotz, for all
their help. I'm so lucky to have so many terrific people in my life!
Thank you all some more.

• • •

This is a work of fiction. Names, characters, places, and incidents are either
products of the author's imagination or, if real, are used fictitiously.

Text copyright © 2016 by N. Griffin
Illustrations copyright © 2016 by Kate Hindley

First edition 2016

Library of Congress Catalog Card Number 2016944083
ISBN 978-0-7636-8535-5

16 17 18 19 20 21 BVG 10 9 8 7 6 5 4 3 2 1

Printed in Berryville, VA, U.S.A.

This book was typeset in Dante.

Candlewick Press
99 Dover Street
Somerville, Massachusetts 02144

visit us at www.candlewick.com

For "Hey, man!" and "It's me!"
N. G.

For Chris
K. H.

CHAPTER 1

The Surprise

It was Monday morning, and Smashie McPerter and her best friend, Dontel Marquise, stood with the rest of their third-grade class at the back of Room 11, jigging excitedly up and down. All last week, their teacher, Ms. Early, had been hinting that a surprise announcement was forthcoming on Monday. And now it *was* Monday, and not only were the members of Room 11 present, but the front of the room was crowded with Room 12 as well—the other third-grade class—still bulky with their not-yet-put-away backpacks. Their very presence suggested that something big was afoot. And from the way Room 12's eyes were bright as they whispered amongst themselves, Smashie could tell that they were as excited about the announcement as she and Dontel and the rest of Room 11 were.

Smashie and Dontel had been best friends practically all their lives. They lived across the street from each other and had so much in common they were more like cousins than just regular best friends. Both loved mathematics and desserts involving plenty of whipped cream but no fruit. They had been the co-champions of both the lower-school spelling bee and the Mathathon last year, titles they hoped to achieve again this year. And they both loved thinking. In fact, their thinking had recently led them to solve a terrible mystery that had plagued Room 11. Patches, the class hamster, had gone missing, and it was only through Smashie and Dontel's intense investigation that he had been recovered and was, even now, wheeling determinedly about in his cage in the back of the room.

"Class!"

The heads of Room 11 whipped round at the call of their teacher.

Ms. Early stood at the front of the room, a sheaf of papers in her hand. "Please finish tidying your things in your cubbies and come to the meeting area."

"Here we go," said Dontel. He glanced at Smashie's hair as she stuffed her hoodie into her cubby.

"I know," said Smashie. "My hair is very sticky-outy today. I combed it and combed it, but it won't calm down."

"Never mind," said Dontel. "The kids are used to your hair being sticky-outy."

"Hey," said Smashie.

"It looks very nice," said Dontel hastily.

"Well, the special announcement will be more important than my hair, I hope," said Smashie. "It must be something super if it involves us and Room 12 together."

"Maybe we're going to finally get to build a rocket!" Dontel wanted to be an astrophysicist when he grew up, and he and Smashie never lost hope that Room 11 would do an astronomy unit in science and a working rocket would be its glorious culmination.

"We could take it out on the athletic fields and let her rip!"

"That would be great!" said Smashie. "Or maybe we are going to start a cookie factory, using recipes of our own invention!"

"Now, that," said Dontel, "would be some kind of good project." The two friends grinned at each other as they headed over to the meeting area.

Smashie and Dontel both loved projects. Dontel liked plans and ideas that took good, deep thinking, and Smashie liked ones with a lot of flair and complications. Their two ways of thinking about things was what made them such a good team.

"We could invent the recipes, and Miss Dismont's class could do the baking," Dontel suggested.

"That wouldn't be fair," said Smashie. "We'd never get a chance to use a mixer." Dontel stayed tactfully silent. Smashie's difficulty with scissors and any kind of machinery with sharp parts was legendary. But she refused to let anybody help her and, consequently, tended to have a lot of Band-Aids on her person. Even now, she had one covered in sparkling stars on her forefinger.

"It also wouldn't be fair not to let Room 12 invent cookies, too," Dontel pointed out. "If you think about it."

"Grark," said Smashie as they arrived at their spots on the meeting rug. But she had to admit that Dontel was right. And besides, it was pretty unlikely that a cookie factory was what the teachers had in mind.

"Make room for Miss Dismont's class," Ms. Early directed as the members of Room 11 started taking their places in their customary circle in the meeting area. "We might have to sit in a double circle today."

"I wonder what the surprise is!" Jacinda Morales said to Joyce Costa as the children sorted themselves out.

"Maybe we're getting a joint class pet to learn about together," said Willette Williams, eyes hopeful. Willette particularly loved Patches, and she was always hoping yet another animal would come to live in Room 11.

"It'd be tricky to share a pet with another class," John Singletary pointed out.

"Not if it's a boa constrictor," said Billy Kamarski. Billy was known for his pranks and over-the-top suggestions. "One of those would be long enough to stretch into both rooms at once!"

"Oooh . . ." breathed Smashie hopefully, but Dontel shuddered. Smashie looked at him in surprise.

"Snakes are slimy," he whispered, tortured.

"No," said Smashie. "That is a myth! Snakes are cool and dry!"

But a joint pet was not the surprise project at all.

"Room 11 and Room 12," said Ms. Early, "Miss Dismont and I know that you are children with a lot of loves and talents. Alonso's singing, for example, and the way Siggie alphabetizes things so quickly. So we came up with an idea."

"A musicale," said Miss Dismont. "A third-grade musicale!"

The children were puzzled.

"What's a musicale?" asked Jacinda.

"Is it us singing?" Smashie asked hopefully. For she loved to sing, and although Smashie did not have the prettiest voice in the class, she certainly had the loudest. By far.

"Partly," said Ms. Early, glancing at Smashie.

"A musicale," Miss Dismont explained, "is a small,

private showcase of talents. Long ago, people had parties at which their guests would take turns performing. In our case, we will invite your families to the school next Wednesday evening, and you will be the ones entertaining them!"

"Yay!" cried Smashie. But a silence filled the rest of the room.

John was the first to break it. "Entertaining them?" he asked skeptically. "Entertaining them how?"

"Well, historically, guests sang, or danced, or spoke pieces for the entertainment of the other guests," said Ms. Early.

"How do you 'speak a piece'?" asked one of the children from Room 12.

"Talk only in fractions, maybe?" wondered another. His name was Carlos, and his eyes brimmed with fun. "One-fourth! One-third! One-half!"

The children laughed. Charlene tilted her head to one side, her eyes on Carlos's curly hair. Jacinda Morales glanced at her and gave a half-grin.

Miss Dismont laughed, too, her own loaf of red hair quivering. Her love for mathematics, including fractions, was well known, and even now she wore her special math brooch—a jeweled kangaroo with silver numbers tumbling out of its pouch like a litter of numerical joeys.

"Speaking pieces is more like reciting a poem, or perhaps a passage from a book you love," she explained.

"So singing, dancing, or speaking is what you want us to do?" asked Siggie.

"Yes, indeed," said Ms. Early.

"Oooh!" cried Smashie. But the other children fell silent again.

"What's the matter?" asked Ms. Early, exchanging a puzzled look with Miss Dismont. "I have to admit, we both thought you'd be very excited."

"Yes," said Miss Dismont. "We thought you would enjoy this opportunity to share what you love doing with your families and friends."

But the students only shifted nervously in their spots in the meeting area.

"Will we have refreshments?" asked Cyrus finally.

"Of course!"

"At least there's that, you all," Cyrus said.

"Cyrus!" said Ms. Early. "I thought you would particularly love this idea."

"I like the part about the refreshments," Cyrus said. "But I don't like the part about doing things in front of people."

"Me, neither," said John immediately.

"Count me out," said Joyce.

"Me too," said Alonso.

Around the circle, there was vigorous nodding.

"I can't stand performing in public," said John. "Makes me all full of bad feelings."

"Really, John?" said Ms. Early. "But I know you have a talent. And we want to show off all our third-grade students."

"You mean all of us have to perform?"

"That's what we mean," Miss Dismont confirmed.

John moaned. His moan was joined by many others.

Smashie glanced from the moaning students to the teachers. Both Miss Dismont and Ms. Early looked almost sad with disappointment. It was too much for

Smashie to bear. Besides, she was gulping with hope. She was never selected to sing in class performances, and here was her chance to volunteer and help her beloved teacher as well.

"I love doing things in front of people," she said stoutly. "*I'll* sing, Ms. Early and Miss Dismont! I have a lot of good ideas about what song I could do." *Something heartfelt,* thought Smashie. *With a lot of parts that are good and loud.*

"Well, Smashie—" Ms. Early paused.

But Smashie had already begun. "*'SMACKED IN THE HEART AND IT'S A SHAME—'CAUSE YOU WON'T TELL ME YOUR NAME'!*" Smashie belted out one of her mother's favorite heavy metal songs.

The children reared back. So did their teachers. The pencils quivered in their containers on the tables.

Smashie stopped, puzzled.

John Singletary took his hands away from his ears. "Are you done?" he asked.

"No," said Smashie. "There's a lot more to that song." And she opened her mouth once more.

"What about speaking a piece, Smashie?" suggested

Ms. Early before Smashie could begin again. "You love to read, and you do it with so much expression. I think you'd have the audience eating out of your hand!"

"What a fine idea!" said Miss Dismont warmly.

"But . . . I was really thinking about singing," said Smashie.

Ms. Early exchanged glances with Miss Dismont. "You certainly do sing loudly," she said.

"With gusto," agreed Miss Dismont, exchanging another glance with Ms. Early, this one slightly more desperate.

"Maybe Smashie should sway in the background while other kids sing," said Billy.

"Billy," said Ms. Early sternly.

Smashie's heart fell. Ms. Early had chastised Billy but had not disagreed with him. And Miss Dismont was already addressing the other children.

"Let's hear from some of the rest of you," she said. "Does anyone else have something they want to do?"

"Music *is* my favorite," said Alonso shyly. "I guess I could sing for the musicale, but only if someone else sings with me, so I don't feel dumb doing it alone."

"I'll sing with you," offered a Room 12 child. Her name was Lilia. "My aunt taught me a song that's real pretty with two people. It's called 'Endless Amour.'"

"I know that one!" said Alonso.

"Super!" said Lilia. "We can do a duet."

"That sounds like a fine idea," said Ms. Early.

Tears pricked at the back of Smashie's eyes. The two teachers were so quick to accept Alonso's idea. Did they really think, as Billy did, that it would be better if Smashie just swayed in the background? Certainly Smashie knew she drowned out many of the other children when they sang as a group, but this would be a solo. They wouldn't even have to give her a microphone. Why, she could be heard at the back of the room even if she didn't have one. And practically no one else was volunteering to perform! She'd have thought Ms. Early would *encourage* her to sing in this instance.

Dontel glanced at her. Smashie knew that he knew how she felt. But before he could say anything, Tatiana broke the silence that had fallen again in Room 11.

"Count me in," she said. "I love to roller-skate, and I know a great song to go with it."

"Wonderful!" said Ms. Early, relieved.

Smashie sat sadly beside Dontel, trying to smooth her unruly hair.

"That's some hair," said John, glancing at her. "But it matches your singing voice."

"Now, John," said Ms. Early warningly.

"I meant it as a compliment," said John hastily. "Smashie is loud, and today her hair looks loud, too."

"You hush," said Smashie, on the verge of tears. This morning was going very badly. "I tried to comb it, but it kept coming out sticky-outy." *And my teacher doesn't like my singing,* she thought, but she didn't say that part out loud.

"Let's get back to our musicale," said Miss Dismont.

Smashie bowed her head and blinked. But the discussion went no further. For Charlene Stott had burst into tears for real.

CHAPTER 2

Charlene's Talent

"Why, Charlene, honey, what's the matter?"

"I don't have a talent," Charlene said, gulping. "Everyone will have something to do but me! I just can't sing, or dance, and I don't have a piece to speak."

"We can help you," said Miss Dismont. "So can your friends. In fact, you should all work together to see what you can contribute."

"But what if we don't even want to do it at all?" said John Singletary.

"I don't think it's fair to make people be in the musicale if they don't want to be," said Cyrus Hull.

"Well, I *do* want to be," sniffled Charlene.

"We will help you if you feel shy," said Ms. Early almost desperately, her arm around Charlene. Despite her broken heart, Smashie looked at Dontel. Even though Ms. Early didn't believe in Smashie's singing voice, her teacher was so excited about the musicale that Smashie couldn't bear to have it ruined for her. And it was terrible to see Charlene so upset. "And, as Miss Dismont said," Ms. Early continued, "you don't have to do it alone. You can have your friends join you."

Like swaying in the background while other people sing, thought Smashie bitterly as she felt a piece of her hair boing up from the cowlick at the back of her head. She tried to smooth it down, but there was no smoothing that cowlick.

"Man, that is some head of hair," said John.

"I *said* I can't *help* it!" said Smashie.

"That was like watching a jack-in-the-box," said Jacinda. "The way it sprang up like that."

"Or like one of those snakes in a can," said Billy. "Which reminds me! I propose a new class pet!"

"Children!" said Ms. Early. "That is enough. You are getting hectic and out of hand. Smashie, your hair looks perfectly fine. Please don't worry about it. And besides," she said with a shudder, "one pet is quite enough."

"Especially when that pet has already caused a lot of upheaval," said Miss Dismont.

Scrabble, scrabble, scrabble, went Patches in his cage.

The noise cheered Smashie despite her misery about the musicale. "That kind of upheaval is right up our alley," she whispered to Dontel.

Dontel nodded. "Yes," he said, "but not upheaval like this with the musicale. No one else likes the idea of performing!"

"I do," said Smashie sadly. Dontel patted her arm.

"Ms. Early, may I help Smashie with her hair?" asked Charlene unexpectedly, wiping away her tears.

"How?" asked Ms. Early.

"I know it's not sharing time, because of the special announcement. But my mother let me bring in something today that might help. Let me show you!" Charlene hurried to her cubby. She came back with an unusual-looking jar in her hand and twisted open its lid. It was filled with a beautiful pale-purple goop.

"What is that?" asked Smashie. Her hair stuck out over her ears like sea kelp.

"Don't be nervous," said Charlene. "This stuff is great."

"Mmm," said Smashie, craning her neck as a lovely scent of lavender and lilacs wafted gently through the room. "Smells good."

"It does smell good," said Charlene. "It's an excellent product. Me and my mom invented it together. She's a professional hair sculptor, and she's striking out on her own to start up a business. She said I could bring a jar in to show everybody. This goop is the secret to our sculpting success! It lengthens and molds the hair into shapes!"

"Permanently?!" said Smashie, clapping her hands on her head.

"No! It washes out. Let me show you what it can do." Charlene got to work. She smoothed the goop into Smashie's hair. She molded and tugged. She whipped and twisted. And after a few minutes, she leaned back to look at her handiwork.

"There," she said. "Done."

And immediately, the two classes, who had been sitting uneasily, worried about what acts they would be forced to perform, burst into grins and excited chatter.

"Wow!" cried Alonso Day.

"Amazing!" shouted a Room 12 child.

"Smashie," said Dontel, "you look A-plus."

Charlene beamed.

"Can I see?" said Smashie. One of the children handed her one of the tiny mirrors the class used when it worked on symmetry and experiments with light. Smashie took a good look at herself. She gasped. Not only was her hair not sticky-outy in its normal way, it was molded into the shape of a music note! What had once been an awful mess on the top of Smashie's head was now a beautifully formed sixteenth note, flags beamed sharply to the side.

"A lucky note," explained Charlene. "To go with the musicale. I was thinking it would give us some ideas."

"It gives me an idea!" shouted a Room 12 child. "Especially if I get a hairdo like that!"

The two teachers exchanged glances. "Charlene," said Ms. Early, "you *do* have a talent. And that talent is hairstyling."

Charlene blushed. "Thank you," she said. "My mom has been teaching me."

"Well, it is a wonderful gift," said Ms. Early.

"Yes," said Miss Dismont.

"But it's not one you can perform," said Charlene.

"But it gives me an idea," said Ms. Early, her eyes sparkling. "Charlene, would you like to design and make special hair sculptures for all the people who agree to perform in the musicale? We would even call the event the Third-Grade Hair Extravaganza and Musicale!"

"Ooh!" breathed some of the children.

"Yes!" said Charlene. "I'd love to." She beamed.

"And do you know what?" Miss Dismont said purposefully. "I bet everyone would enjoy a hair sculpture like that."

"Yes!"

"I would!

"Me too!"

"Hurrah!" cried Charlene. "I just know I can help us all look great!"

"Hold on a second, Ms. Early and Miss Dismont," said John. "Are you all saying that we can only get our hair sculpted into a cool shape if we agree to participate in the musicale?"

"That," said Ms. Early firmly, "is exactly what we're saying."

Several members of the two classes exchanged frantic glances. Smashie knew some children still felt too shy to perform. But the idea of having their hair sculpted into something amazing to match their act . . .

Then Smashie remembered. She wouldn't have her own act. She would be swaying in the background while Alonso or somebody else sang. And as glad as she was that Charlene felt better, Smashie wasn't sure that even a musical hair note could make up for that kind of disappointment.

CHAPTER 3

Hair Ideas

"Will Alonso and I get neat hair sculptures like that, then?" asked Lilia eagerly.

"You bet," said Miss Dismont.

"I could do Tatiana's hair in a roller skate," cried Charlene. "To go along with her song! I can do anything!"

So can I, thought Smashie. *Singing-wise. But the teachers won't let me.* Maybe she could talk to Ms. Early privately, after the meeting.

Tatiana squirmed with happy anticipation. "Ms.

Early, can Charlene do roller-skate hair on me right now?"

"She certainly can," said Ms. Early with a smile in Miss Dismont's direction.

Rubbing her hands with the purple goop, Charlene got to work. And now Tatiana was the one who was transformed. Where there had once been a tumble of dark curls there was now a perfect roller skate of hair sitting atop Tatiana's head.

"Wow!"

"Amazing!"

"Ms. Early," asked John desperately, "what if we just can't do it? I just can't stand performing in public!"

Indeed, faint cries of unwilling children were heard here and there throughout the meeting area. But even more were looking at Smashie's and Tatiana's heads, and Smashie knew they were on the edge of changing their minds. And she was right. Suddenly, lots of kids had ideas for acts. Several children volunteered to be backup dancers for the performers. Siggie, changing his mind perhaps the most abruptly of all, offered to do an act wherein he alphabetized some items very quickly.

"Can you do a cool hair sculpture to match that?" Siggie asked Charlene.

"You bet!" said Charlene. "I could make your hair into an ABC!"

"Yes!" said Tatiana. "And his backup singers could sing the alphabet in English *and* Spanish!"

"And I could alphabetize the objects in both languages!" cried Siggie.

"Terrific!" said Miss Dismont, scribbling madly on a piece of chart paper.

"This is not terrific!" It was John, and his face was stormy. "I feel blackmailed! I want cool hair, but I have to perform to get it?"

And here's me not even going to get to belt out a single note, thought Smashie sadly.

But before either teacher could respond, Charlene held up her hand.

"It's not just the teachers that are setting a limit, John."

"What do you mean?"

"The ingredients that my mom uses to make this stuff are really expensive. She told me last night that she only has enough left to make about two more jars. Each jar has enough goop for about fifteen heads. Both our classes have nineteen students in them. With the two jars she can make, plus this one I have here, there is just about enough to do everyone's hair for the musicale. And there's a little extra for me to practice with—or in case I mess up."

"Why doesn't your mom just buy more ingredients?" asked Siggie.

"Because"—Charlene bit her lip—"because it's hard starting your own business. We can't afford to buy more ingredients right now."

"Oh," said Smashie. "That makes sense."

Jacinda gave Charlene's shoulders a side hug.

"I'll speak a piece," Dontel volunteered. "There's a passage I love from one of my favorite astronomy books."

Smashie looked at him, betrayed. He gave her a meaningful look back. "Better to volunteer now," he whispered to her, "before they find out what we can *really* do."

And Smashie, shocked, subsided. For she knew Dontel was right. She hadn't even thought about their secret talent, and by that unfortunately she didn't mean investigating. Even if she wasn't allowed to sing, *anything* was better than being forced to do their secret talent. Smashie had better think fast if they were going to come up with a surefire way to avoid that. Dontel looked at her and they nodded once, together. They were agreed.

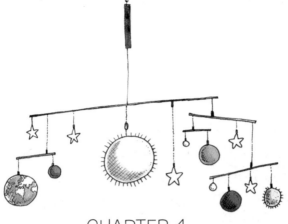

CHAPTER 4

Planning with Goop

One eye on John, who had fled to his seat, Ms. Early said, "I'm so pleased some of you children are getting excited. Charlene, we will buy all three jars from your mother. We can pay for them out of the funds we've raised so far for our class trip to the planetarium."

Smashie and Dontel exchanged alarmed glances. They had been looking forward to the field trip to the planetarium for some time. It was the spark they were hoping for to start that unit on astronomy.

"We can have some kind of bake sale and re-raise the rest of the money later," Ms. Early said, and Smashie and Dontel breathed sighs of relief.

"I bet our musicale will be great for your mom's new business, Charlene," said Smashie.

"Yes," agreed Dontel. "I bet people will see our hairdos and hustle right over there."

"Do you really think so, Dontel?" asked Charlene, some of the worn look fading from her face.

"Well, I do," said Jacinda. "Who wouldn't want hair sculptures like ours?"

"My mom's are even better!" cried Charlene. "If business picked up, she could afford to make more of the special goop, and her new company would be off and running." Charlene was positively smiling now.

"That's what we mean, Charlene!" said Dontel.

"I can't wait for next Wednesday!" Siggie was as enthusiastic about the musicale now as he had been suspicious of it before.

"None of us can," said Ms. Early. "And I mean that literally as well as figuratively. We only have nine days to get ready, including the weekend. That means that you children should choose to perform things that you already know well, since our rehearsal time is so short."

"Does the goop work on all kinds of hair, Charlene?" asked Willette.

"Yes," said Charlene. "My mom made sure while we were inventing it. It works on all kinds of hair."

"Hooray!" shouted Rooms 11 and 12.

Carlos opened his mouth, then closed it. He blushed again. "Your hairstyles will be great, Charlene," he said.

But Charlene was too excited to hear him. She bounced up and down happily. Smashie was glad for her. She knew how worried Charlene had been, and this new idea was bound to help—not only with the musicale, but with Charlene's mother's new business as well. But what could Smashie think of to do for the musicale besides sway, like Billy had said?

"May I see the jar of goop?" asked Jacinda. "I want to smell it up close."

Charlene passed the jar over. "It's called Herr Goop," she said.

"Hair Goop?" asked John.

"No, *Herr* Goop. *Herr* means Mister in German, but

it's pronounced like we say 'hair.' My mom thought it'd be funny."

"A homophone," said Dontel. "But in a foreign language. It *is* funny."

"My grammy calls that a double meaning," said Smashie, and once again the children looked her way with her music note head. They beamed. Smashie beamed back. She had to admit, the hair music symbol did make her feel a little better.

HERR · GOOP

Let a little German help you lengthen and mold your hair into beautiful sculptures

"You can send the goop around the circle as we plan, so everybody can have a sniff," said Ms. Early. "And we'll write everyone's ideas on this piece of chart paper."

"I stink at singing and dancing," moaned Cyrus. "I get all muddled up trying to keep with the beat. Can't I just be in charge of refreshments?"

"You may certainly be in charge of refreshments," said Miss Dismont. "But we expect every third-grader to take part in the musicale."

At his seat, John raised his head from the table and let it clonk down in despair.

Smashie and Dontel exchanged concerned looks. Normally, John was one of the toughest, bravest kids in the class. But the idea of performing seemed to suck all the bravery out of him.

Joyce passed the Herr Goop jar to Dontel, who studied the bottle and breathed in the scent of its contents before he handed it to Smashie.

"Mmmm. This Herr Goop really does smell wonderful," said Smashie. She looked up. *Maybe if Dontel could speak a piece, she could be allowed to sing as well?*

But before she could muster the courage to ask once again if she could sing, Billy Kamarski was already speaking.

"I have a great idea," he said. "I'll sing 'Machine Gun Jailbreak'!"

"NO," said both teachers at once.

"Absolutely not," said Ms. Early.

"Completely inappropriate," said Miss Dismont.

"Aw, come on," said Billy. "Please?"

The teachers looked at him silently.

"Oh, fine," said Billy. "Squash my dreams."

Welcome to the club, thought Smashie.

The bell rang.

"Time for PE, Room 11," said Ms. Early.

"And time for Room 12 to go back to our room," said Miss Dismont. "I think we have a good head of steam going with this. I'm very excited!"

"We are, too!" said a couple of children.

"Can't wait!" cried several more.

But John, once again, said, "Ugh."

"Hey," said Charlene, "can I have my jar of goop back?"

"Of course," said Ms. Early. "Who has it?"

Everybody looked at everybody else. But no one had the jar.

"It must have rolled away, Charlene," said Ms. Early. "Let's have a quick cleanup now and see if we can't uncover it. Speedy, now."

The children tidied and looked, but no one found the jar.

"Maybe someone took it," said Joyce.

"Darn," said Charlene, her eyes scanning the room. "Thank you for looking, Ms. Early and everybody. That goop costs my mom so much to make I don't want to lose any of it. She told me I could bring it to school only if I was real careful with it. Plus, we need it now, to have enough for the Hair Extravaganza and Musicale."

"We'll all keep looking for it," said Smashie, who lost things often and knew how Charlene must be feeling.

"Thanks, Smash."

"Now, let's line up and file, children." And Ms. Early led them to the gym.

Who knew that the missing jar of Herr Goop would set off a whirl of intrigue and mystery that would plunge Room 11 into chaos and suspicion not seen since the disappearance of Patches? Who knew that Smashie and Dontel would once again have to assume the role of investigators? Nobody.

Yet.

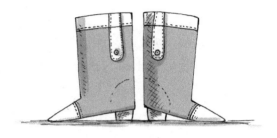

CHAPTER 5

A Dread Realized

Grammy and Dr. Marquise were waiting at the open door when Mr. Potter let Smashie and Dontel off the bus.

"I wonder why your dad is at my house at this hour," said Smashie.

"Me too," said Dontel. Usually his father's dental practice kept him at work until suppertime.

But not today. The children could tell that Dr. Marquise was bursting with news. So was Smashie's grammy, standing beside him.

"Guess who just called?" asked Grammy as they entered the house.

"Bon Jovi?" asked Smashie hopefully.

"No," said Dr. Marquise.

But Dontel knew.

"Ms. Early," he said.

"Yes!" said Dr. Marquise. "How did you know?"

"Just a feeling," said Dontel.

"And do you know what she told me about?"

Smashie drooped. "The musicale," she said dully.

"Exactly. And she asked me if you had any other talents besides your singing," said Grammy.

Smashie moaned in despair.

"Your wonderful, loud singing," Dr. Marquise added hastily.

"And do you know what I told her?" said Grammy.

The children did not have to guess.

Smashie looked at Dontel. Dontel looked at Smashie. They knew the power of will their relatives had. There would be no choice. Smashie would not sing in the musicale. Instead, her teacher, her grandmother, and Dr. Marquise would force her and Dontel to perform what Grammy and Dontel's dad had been teaching them since they were three. Their secret talent.

Sixties go-go dancing.

The music note on the top of Smashie's head quivered.

CHAPTER 6
Forced

"Sixties go-go dances are perfect for your musicale!" said Dr. Marquise, who was something of a dance historian on the side. "The other kids will have a blast when you teach them the easy moves and the fun names for the dances. Let's get to it! We could do the Twist! Then the Pony!" Still wearing his white coat, Dr. Marquise rolled up his sleeves and was clearly set for action. He led them all into the living room. Smashie and Dontel drooped as they followed him. They knew what was coming next. Never mind the rolled-up rug and the record player ready to go; there were also pictures all over the walls: Smashie and Dontel in preschool with matching costumes and go-go boots. Smashie and Dontel in kindergarten, performing at a function for Dontel's church in hats designed by Dr. Marquise. And there was one from just last year, as they performed, in sparkly jumpsuits, for their grandmothers' detective-novel book club.

"It's our worst fear realized," said Dontel. "And to think I thought speaking a piece would forestall it."

"Nope," muttered Smashie. "Not if our teacher got to them. Nothing can save us now."

"Come on, kids!" said Smashie's grammy. "Let's get going! Dr. Marquise came home early from work specially to rehearse! You two are going to be the hit of that musicale!" Her eyes were bright with excitement, for Grammy loved sixties go-go dancing. "Makes me relive my youth," she always said. Go-go dancing had been popular in the 1960s, when Grammy was a girl.

"It'll be great!" cried Dr. Marquise. "Every act is going to be punctuated by your specialty! So we better get going and get you kids back into form!"

Smashie blinked back tears. But Grammy, not noticing, pushed PLAY on the stereo. "We'll start off easy. Get you warmed up."

And she and Dr. Marquise began to do the Twist, twisting their torsos back and forth while their legs shifted in the opposite direction.

"Come on, Dontel! Put some life in it!" cried Dr. Marquise, kicking one of his legs to the side.

Dontel put some life in it.

"Smashie! Twist like you mean it."

Reluctantly, Smashie tried to twist like she meant it. "Grammy," she puffed, "Dontel and I have a lot of work to do. Can't we practice later?"

"Yeah," said Dontel. "We have to do some . . ." He caught Smashie's eye. She knew that he knew how she was feeling about all this — the phone call, the not-singing, this forced dance rehearsal — "homework."

"You can do your homework later!" shouted Dr. Marquise. "Come on, Sue, let's give them a go at the Swim!" And, as the music changed, he began flinging his arms in swooping swimming motions and boinged about the room.

Dontel groaned. But he dutifully arm-swam across the room.

"Let's partner for this one," said Dr. Marquise. "I think it'd be nice to have the kids in pairs. Smashie, watch what I do."

"Dontel, watch me," ordered Grammy.

And, with Smashie and Dontel following their assigned grown-ups, the impromptu dancing continued.

CHAPTER 7

Dealing
with
Disappointment

It was terrible. And there was no stopping Ms. Early, either. The two classes met again during morning meeting the next day. "I happen to have found out about another talent we have in our third grade," Ms. Early said to everybody, out loud. "A wonderful talent that brings a smile to the face of everyone who watches Dontel and Smashie perform."

"It's not a talent," said Smashie, sinking down until she was practically sitting on her neck against the bookcase. "It's just a thing the two of them make us do."

"Yes," said Dontel. "They force us because they're the ones who love it."

"Who?" asked Carlos.

"My grammy," said Smashie.

"And my dad," said Dontel.

"What do they make you do?"

Ms. Early explained as Smashie and Dontel slunk lower and lower in their spots. "And just as Smashie and Dontel say," she continued, "we're lucky enough to have in our parent—and grandparent—body two fine dancers who have agreed to prepare Smashie and Dontel to teach you children sixties go-go dances to perform between our other numbers!"

It was clear as she beamed at Smashie that Ms. Early felt this made up for the singing.

It did not.

Humiliated, Smashie bent her head sadly as more of the children told their teachers what acts they wanted to perform and were granted permission to do as they wished. Their families had not gotten phone calls about how terrible they were. Apparently, that was just Smashie.

Smashie's mother had understood. "I know you want to sing," she had said last night after Dontel and Dr. Marquise left and Smashie explained about the day and the music note on the top of her head. "But we can't always get what we want. I'm so sorry about it this time. And you know those heavy metal songs by heart."

"I do," said Smashie, her tears breaking through at last. Her mother put her arms around her.

"What about a suit?" she asked. For Smashie was well known for the suits she created to help herself get in the right frame of mind to solve difficult problems. She had made an Investigator Suit, for example, to solve the mystery of Patches's disappearance (one of her grammy's old hot-suits with a sash full of pouches for clues). And just last week it had been necessary to create a Find Where I Put the Mail I Brought from the Mailbox Suit. (This suit consisted of a hastily made blue-crayoned cardboard carton with eyeholes, to help Smashie feel like a mailbox. The Band-Aid on her forefinger right now was a result of cutting out those eyeholes.) A Choreographer Suit with some kind of in-charge-looking shirt and a go-go boot of hair might be just the things to take some of the sting out of her disappointment at not getting to sing in the musicale.

"I'll help you," said Mrs. McPerter. "Let's get started right now. We'll make the best Choreographer Suit you can imagine!"

And they had gotten out their hot-glue gun and got to work. It helped. Not so much the suit, this time, but just knowing that her mother was on her side.

Now, in the meeting area, Smashie gently touched her fraying hair musical note as she tried to cheer herself with thoughts of her still-under-construction Choreographer Suit while the other children talked about their numbers for the Hair Extravaganza and Musicale.

"At least Charlene is happy," she whispered to Dontel. He nodded. For Charlene was transformed since yesterday, her cheeks pink with ideas and happiness.

"There's still time to add numbers," said Ms. Early. "So if any of you think of something you want to do for the musicale, don't hesitate to tell me or write me a note."

Smashie popped up her head. If they still needed acts, should she ask again if she could sing? She pictured herself, in a wonderful costume that was even better than a Choreographer Suit, singing a foot-stomping version of "Smacked in the Heart" in front of her friends and their families. But she knew Ms. Early would not say yes.

Billy said, "I still want to do 'Machine Gun Jailbreak.'"

Ms. Early quelled him with a look.

John said, "I still want to sit at home and forget this whole thing."

"Why do you hate the idea of performing so much?" asked Dontel.

"Because I don't like looking stupid! Up there in front of everybody with my neck looking weird, singing some dumb song and all the grown-ups laughing!"

"What do you mean about your neck?" asked Smashie, puzzled.

"It just feels that way," said John, fingering his collar at the thought. "When I sing."

"That's not how it will be, I don't think," said Dontel. "I think our families are on our side. They'll probably just clap."

"Sure," said John miserably. "And take a million pictures, and before you know it, they're passing them around at Thanksgiving and everyone is laughing at your neck. No, thank you. I am not down with this musicale."

"John, you and I can talk about this later," said Ms. Early. "It is almost time for language arts."

"What about the goop?" asked Tatiana. "Did you find it after we left yesterday, Ms. Early?"

"I'm afraid I didn't," said Ms. Early, her face concerned. "But let's not worry yet. Things have a way of turning up."

"Do you think maybe it was swiped?" asked Joyce.

"Certainly not," said Ms. Early. "Just because of Patches, you children think everything—"

"I sure hope it wasn't," Charlene said worriedly. "Still, my mom made our next jar of Herr Goop last night, and I brought it in."

"Yay!" cried Room 11, minus John.

"Will you test it on me?" asked Joyce.

"We don't want to waste it, do we?" asked Ms. Early.

"It's okay," said Charlene. "I'll just use a tiny dab on Joyce."

And after a few minutes and some smears of the beautifully scented product, a plump heart made of Joyce's hair rose proudly from the top of her head.

"Because you said on the bus you wanted to back up Alonso and Lilia in 'Endless Amour,'" said Charlene. "And 'amour' is French for love. This will look great, right?"

Cyrus handed Joyce one of the little mirrors.

Joyce beamed.

"I look super!" she cried.

"You do!" cried Alonso. "We'd love to have you back up our song!"

"It looks wonderful!"

"You got a gift, Charlene."

"Our musicale is going to be the best ever with this cool hair!"

Room 11, minus John, was thrilled. Joyce's heart hair looked as good as Smashie's music note had—at least yesterday, when it was fresh. And so the class continued somewhat more happily until recess.

CHAPTER 8

Accidental Insults

Everybody was outside. Smashie was not at her best with athletic things, so she and Dontel often separated at recess. Right now, he and a lot of the other children were playing a vigorous game of tag on the grass beyond the blacktop while Smashie reluctantly agreed to play catch with Joyce, Tatiana, and Cyrus.

Jacinda and Charlene were over by the play-equipment bag, whispering furiously.

"I think Charlene likes Carlos," Joyce confided to the other children as they headed over to get a ball.

"I think Carlos likes Charlene," said Tatiana.

"Why shouldn't they like each other?" asked Smashie. "Most all of us do."

"We mean, like, like-like, Smashie," said Tatiana.

"*Like-like?* We are only in the third grade!"

"Well, we had that awful thing where Mr. Carper, the sub, like-liked our teacher," Cyrus reminded her.

"I don't think he did," said Smashie. "And he wasn't a third-grader. Besides, Charlene and Jacinda look too thoughtful to be talking about like-liking anyone."

"They're probably talking about ways to help Charlene's mom build her business," said Joyce. But Smashie noticed that the girls kept sneaking peeks over to the tag game. Normally, Charlene and Jacinda

would be playing tag, too — they were both excellent runners. And their gaze certainly was focused on Carlos. There might be something to this like-like theory after all.

Carlos was a beautiful runner as well.

"Hey, you two," said Joyce to the girls as they reached the play-equipment bag. "We're going to play catch. Want to join us?"

"Sure," said Jacinda.

Charlene nudged Jacinda's arm.

"What?"

"I thought we were planning about looking for my Herr Goop jar!"

"We will," said Jacinda. "Don't worry."

"I *am* worried," Charlene confessed. "I'm worried someone took it!"

"Who'd do that? You already offered it to the whole grade for the musicale, for Pete's sake," said Cyrus, tossing the ball to Joyce, who caught it. "Plus, no one else knows how to sculpt hair."

"Maybe you're right," said Charlene, catching the ball from Joyce. "It's just that my mom is mad at me for losing a whole jar of goop. And we won't have enough for the musicale if I can't find it." She tossed the ball to Smashie, who promptly dropped it.

PHWEET!

It was the yard lady's whistle. "You go get that ball before someone breaks a leg!" she shouted. Smashie ran and got the ball.

"We have to have enough goop!" cried Joyce as Smashie returned. "Otherwise our Hair Extravaganza and Musicale will be like just any other old show!"

The children were worried. A distraction was needed.

"Why don't I show you all some sixties go-go dancing?" said Smashie.

"Yes!" said Cyrus. "I need to see what it looks like for real. I hope it's easy to learn."

"Oh, it is," said Smashie. "We can do a funny one. It's called the Jerk!"

"The Jerk?" said Cyrus.

"Yep," said Smashie.

"Show us," Jacinda demanded, and the whole group of children fell in behind Smashie.

"It's a lot with your arms. Like this." Smashie shimmied down the blacktop, her arms flinging

themselves one at a time over her head. "Bomp! Bomp, bomp! Bomp, bomp, bomp, bomp!" sang Smashie as she flung. The others followed in her wake.

PHWEET! The yard lady again. "Smashie McPerter! WHAT ARE YOU DOING?"

"It's the Jerk, Miss Martone!"

"WHAT DID YOU CALL ME?"

"I—"

"Off the blacktop!"

"But I wasn't saying you were a—"

"OFF!"

Smashie sighed and made her way to the edge of the blacktop where children stood to be punished. The other kids waved sadly to her. "Sorry, Smash!" called Joyce. The others looked sympathetic. But they daren't practice the dance now. Only Charlene looked preoccupied, watching the tag game out of the corner of her eye.

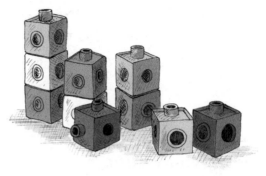

CHAPTER 9

Smashie in Trouble

"Can I smell the goop again?" asked Smashie as they came in from recess at last and got ready for math class.

"Sure," said Charlene, and tossed the new jar she had brought in that morning gently in Smashie's direction.

"Don't throw things!" cried Ms. Early.

"Especially to Smashie!" Cyrus implored even as Dontel reached up and caught the jar before it hit the table. Smashie opened her mouth to protest, but then shut it again. Cyrus was right. She was terrible at catching things.

"Phew," went the class.

Dontel inspected the label on the jar and said, "Herr Goop. I really like that name," before he passed the jar over to Smashie, who looked at it closely herself before she opened it to inhale its lovely, light scent. Today there was a serial number on the jar under the picture of the little German. *I bet Charlene's mom decided to put numbers on there to keep track of it after the first one got lost,* thought Smashie.

"Let's get to our math," said Ms. Early. "I'm thinking about the number 67. How many tens in that number?"

"Six!" the children called out.

"And how many ones left over?"

"Seven!"

"How could you prove it to me?"

"I wonder how Charlene will do *our* hair for the dances," Dontel said as he broke the numbers Ms. Early was listing on the whiteboard into tens and ones.

"Well," said Smashie, looking at the blank spaces on Ms. Early's musicale chart, "I know one dance we won't do."

And, as if on cue, the door to Room 11 slammed open, and in its frame stood Mrs. Armstrong, principal of the Rebecca Lee Crumpler Elementary School.

"ROOM 11! I am JUST SICK! What is all this I hear about Smashie McPerter calling our yard lady a jerk?"

"Oh, dear!" said Ms. Early. "Smashie, what do you have to say for yourself? You know we do *not* call people names in Room 11!"

"I wasn't calling her a name!" said Smashie desperately. "It's the name of a sixties dance! I was showing the kids!"

"Tchah!" said Mrs. Armstrong.

"It's true," said Cyrus earnestly, backing her up. "We wanted Smashie to demonstrate, and that was the name of the dance."

Ms. Early looked relieved. "I'm afraid this is my fault, Mrs. Armstrong," she said. "Smashie and Dontel are teaching the children sixties go-go dances for our musicale, and I did ask them to help the other children learn them. I think Miss Martone misunderstood. I'll speak to her myself."

"I will, too," said Smashie earnestly.

"Hmph," said Mrs. Armstrong.

"But we certainly won't be performing . . . that particular dance, will we, Smashie and Dontel? Just in case we insult someone?" said Ms. Early.

"No, Ms. Early," said Smashie and Dontel in unison.

"Certainly not," said Mrs. Armstrong. "Why, I'D BE SICK IN BED WITH A CONTAINER OF MEDICINE BESIDE ME if you were to dance, or even discuss, that number!"

"Actually," said Smashie, seizing the moment, "if you'd rather I sang—"

"Excuse me, boss." Mr. Bloom, the head custodian, appeared in the doorway and nodded at Mrs. Armstrong. "Got the empty recycling containers for you, Ms. E." He glanced at the chart at the front of the room. "That's a good-lookin' list of acts for your musicale. Looking forward to the sixties dances myself. You know what one was my favorite? Called the Jerk. I remember I was pretty good at that one." And he set down the recycling containers and left the room, flinging his arms over his head one by one and humming "The Jerk," a song made popular by the Larks long ago.

Mrs. Armstrong wilted in the doorway.

"*Hey!*" Charlene shouted, before the conversation could continue. "What happened to my new jar of goop? It's gone!"

CHAPTER 10

Disappearance!

"Another one? Gone?" Cyrus's voice was incredulous.

"We'll never be able to do our Hair Extravaganza and Musicale now!" cried Joyce. "Not with just dumb regular ungooped hair!"

And the class rang with shouts of agreement and despair.

"It can't be!" cried Joyce. "How could both jars just disappear?"

"Magic," breathed Smashie.

"Sure," said John sarcastically. "There's a wizard

going around wanting to sculpt himself a heck of a hairdo. High and tight, maybe. Or a bowl cut."

But Smashie's mind was off to the races. *A wizard's hairdo! Gray hair poking out all scraggy-like, frizzy, and full of secrets!*

"Smashie," said Dontel.

With a great effort, Smashie pulled herself away from her wizardly imaginings. Because she knew what Dontel meant. One jar of Herr Goop could roll away. But two . . . ?

"Too much of a coincidence," Dontel whispered to Smashie. "Something is up."

He and Smashie locked eyes and nodded.

"We are going to have to investigate," said Smashie.

The scent of lavender and lilacs filled the room.

CHAPTER 11
Mad at Ms. Early?

Even though Joyce and her hair heart had left after lunch for an orthodontist appointment, the hair goop scent filled the hallway as the children lined up to go home at the end of the day. Apparently Herr Goop was potent-smelling stuff.

"Don't forget to practice your acts, those of you who've signed up," Ms. Early called as they filed to the buses. "Just six school days until our musicale!"

"I'm afraid we won't be ready," Tatiana fretted.

"I'm afraid Ms. Early's going to force me to do it,

period," said John. "It's unfair! Isn't this a free country? Do I really have to perform when I don't want to?"

"But those cool hair sculptures," said Tatiana. "Don't you want one, too?"

John hesitated. Then he shook his head. "I have got to remain strong about this. I never thought the day would come when I'd be mad at Ms. Early, but here it is."

Smashie's heart sank. When would not being allowed to sing in the musicale stop making her feel so terrible? And worse yet, if she was honest with herself, she and John were as one. Smashie was mad at Ms. Early, too.

Mad at Ms. Early? Her most favorite teacher that she and Dontel had so far? What if Smashie stopped liking her for the whole rest of the year?

"Dontel," whispered Smashie, "what if I never forgive Ms. Early?"

"First things first," Dontel said firmly to Smashie. "You know what we're doing when we get home, right?"

"Investigating the missing Herr Goop," said Smashie. She couldn't be the one to bring Room 11 down even more, despite her feeling so sad. She had to help find that goop. "I still have our notebooks from last time. And my Investigator Suit."

"Yes," said Dontel. "But what we have first is our rehearsal. With your grammy."

"And your dad."

"Yeech."

"Yes," said Smashie. "Yeech."

CHAPTER 12

Motion Sparks the Notion

"Finally," said Smashie. "We can do some investigator thinking." At last they'd been released from dance practice by the adults. The slate of dances had been agreed upon, and Smashie and Dontel had promised to continue to practice on their own. "We have one heck of a hard problem. If we don't find that hair goop, all the kids who are only doing the musicale because they're going to get a cool hairstyle will drop out again!"

"Yes," agreed Dontel. "And Ms. Early will be devastated."

"So will the people who really do want to perform. Like Siggie and his alphabetizing." Trying hard not to think that Ms. Early and the other performers weren't the only people who were or would be devastated about the musicale, Smashie got up. "I better get my Investigator Suit on."

"You can wear that suit now, Smashie," said Dontel. "But don't wear it to school tomorrow. The kids all know that was your Investigator Suit from the Patches time. We don't want to put anyone on guard."

Smashie's jaw dropped. "You are right!" she cried. "Because clearly the goop taker *is in our class!*"

"Clearly," said Dontel. "But let's not get ahead of ourselves. We need our Investigation Notebooks."

"I have them right here in the credenza," said Smashie, and fished them out. She handed Dontel his, which said FIRST STREET BAPTIST on it. Her own featured a very thoughtful horse.

"Forget my suit," said Smashie. "Let's get started."

REASONS WHY WE THINK THE PERP IS IN OUR CLASS, wrote the two friends in their notebooks.

"It's very exciting to be using Investigator Language like *perp* again!" said Smashie. *Perp* was short for "perpetrator," which meant a person who had committed a crime. During the Patches investigation, the two friends had devoted a whole part of the back of their Investigation Notebooks to record the various new investigator words they used. They glanced fondly at that list now.

"Let's think it through," said Dontel, flipping back to their current page. "We need to be logical and back up our ideas."

"Just like mathematicians," Smashie agreed, nodding. "Well, both times the goop disappeared while we were all right there in class," she pointed out. "That was pretty slick of the perpetrator."

"Yes," agreed Dontel. "Let's write down what you just said as a reason for our thinking the thief is a member of Room 11 or Room 12," said Dontel.

> 1. Because we were all in the room and it disappeared right under our noses and only third-graders were in the room because of course it is not Ms. Early or Miss Dismont.

"That's a good start," said Dontel. "And we also think it because the person had to be in the meeting circle when the first jar went missing. And also in our class at math time when the second one disappeared."

"You mean the thief had *opportunity!*" cried Smashie.

"More Investigator Language!" Dontel said. Both added *opportunity* to their lists. "Let's make a list of things that have to be true about the thief and his or her opportunity."

"Ooh," said Smashie pleasurably.

THINGS THAT MUST BE TRUE ABOUT THE
PERSON, LIKE OPPORTUNITY
1. They had to be in the musicale planning
meeting circle because that's when the first jar
of goop went missing.
2. They had to be in math when we did the
tens and ones review because that is when the
second jar of goop went missing.

"Dontel!" said Smashie. "That means the perp is

in our class and not a member of Room 12! Because Room 12 wasn't in math with us!"

"Good thinking, Smash! Do we have another fact that should be on this list that could narrow things down even more?" Dontel asked.

Smashie thought. "Not really," she said after a moment. "I think that's pretty much the size of it. Two swipes of goop; two opportunities."

"Fine," said Dontel. "Let's get to thinking about suspects, then."

"Suspects!" Smashie cried. *Suspects* was already on the Investigator Language page as well, but Smashie took the opportunity to underline it before she and Dontel started a fresh page in their notebooks.

SUSPECT LIST

"Hmm," said Dontel. "I don't like it when we have to suspect class members. We really do have a very nice class."

"Yes," said Smashie. "We do."

"I have no idea who to even start with," Dontel admitted.

"Me, either," said Smashie.

"Everyone in our whole class had both those opportunities."

"Yes."

"Well," said Dontel, "like Ms. Early always says, if you have a hard problem, move! Motion can spark a notion! We might as well try."

"Yes," Smashie agreed. "And this sure is a hard problem. Let's dance on it."

Necks bobbing, Smashie and Dontel did the Funky Chicken across the room.

"It has to be someone who loves the goop," Smashie puffed.

"Could be," Dontel puffed back. He added wingy arm motions and started back across the room. "Maybe someone who likes the smell."

"Or wants their hair in shapes," Smashie said. "Though everybody in the third grade is excited about having our hair in shapes. Even the teachers think it's going to make our Hair Extravaganza and Musicale something really special. We can't investigate every single third-grader, can we?"

"No." Dontel sighed. "We have to trim it down. Let's dance!"

And they began to do the Nitty Gritty in earnest.

But soon Dontel stopped. "I've got an idea!" he said. "Instead of starting with the list of suspects, why don't we make a list of reasons *why* people would steal the goop? We just thought of a bunch. And that technique really helped us with the Patches investigation. If we find a solid *motive*, we can figure out the perp!"

Smashie, delighted with Investigator Language like *motive*, was immediately on board.

The two flung themselves down on their stomachs and started yet another page.

MOTIVES WHY SOMEONE WOULD WANT
TO TAKE THE GOOP

1. They want their hair always lengthened
and in shapes.

"That makes sense," said Dontel. "Maybe it's someone who doesn't want to wait until the musicale for his or her hair to be in a shape."

"Dontel," said Smashie, "that is all of us."

"Good point," said Dontel.

"Wait a minute," said Smashie. "*Is* it all of us? What if it's the opposite? What if it's someone who *doesn't* want their hair lengthened and molded?"

"What do you mean?"

"I mean, everyone is very excited now about having cool hair for the musicale. But some people," she said, "don't like the idea of a Hair Extravaganza and Musicale at all!"

"*John!*" shouted Dontel. "He hates the musicale! He thinks we will look dumb!"

"Exactly," said Smashie. "And if he steals the goop, maybe he believes it will sabotage the show."

"Or that we will lose heart and cancel," said Dontel.

"Yes," said Smashie. "Either way."

They added to the Motives List.

1. They want their hair always lengthened and in shapes.
2. They want to sabotage the musicale!

And to the Suspect List they added:

1. John

"I feel peculiar putting John on the list," Smashie admitted. "He is a good friend of ours."

"I know," said Dontel. "But think what our grandmas say about the detectives in those books they read all the time. You can't let your feelings blind you to the possibilities."

"Ugh," said Smashie, who rather liked having her feelings blind her to possibilities.

"Is there anyone else who you think would want to sabotage the musicale?" asked Dontel. "I mean, there are kids who are on the fence about performing, but I can't think of another person who's as against it as John."

"You're right," said Smashie. She thought. "I can't think of any other motives, either." She paused. "Except maybe Ms. Early," she said darkly. "She doesn't want *everybody* to have fun doing the musicale."

"Smashie," said Dontel, "be fair. You and I are leading all of the dances. We are doing more for the musicale than anybody."

Smashie began to scowl. But then the truth of her feelings came through, and the corners of her mouth turned down. "I know," she said. "I just really want to sing."

"What if you hum a few bars around Ms. Early when you get a chance?" Dontel suggested. "Kind of quietly, like you're just humming while you're thinking. Maybe then she'll get the idea to give you a chance to sing a song."

"Dontel," said Smashie, "that is a wonderful idea. I'm going to do it!"

"Great!" said Dontel. "Now do you think you

can concentrate on our investigation about the hair goop?"

"I sure can," said Smashie. "Let's dance on it again!"

And they had barely begun to do the Swim when Smashie shouted, "I've got it!"

"What?" cried Dontel.

"Billy," said Smashie firmly.

"But he loves to perform," said Dontel.

"Yes," said Smashie, "but he is super mad the teachers won't let him sing 'Machine Gun Jailbreak'!"

"Completely inappropriate," Dontel said, remembering.

"Exactly," said Smashie. "And if he can't sing what he wants, I bet he wants to wreck the whole thing for everybody!"

"Motive!" cried Dontel. "Same motive—sabotage—but for a different reason in Billy's case. Smashie, we are really good investigators."

"I know," said Smashie smugly as they added to the Motives List.

1. They want their hair always lengthened and in shapes.

2. They want to sabotage the musicale!
3. They are mad they can't sing "Machine Gun Jailbreak."

And to the Suspect List they added:

1. John
2. Billy

"Also, we always have to consider what a prankster Billy is," Smashie pointed out. "He might just think it's a great joke."

"True enough. Let's add that to the Motives List."

1. They want their hair always lengthened and in shapes.
2. They want to sabotage the musicale!
3. They are mad they can't sing "Machine Gun Jailbreak."
4. They think it is a funny joke.

Dontel thwapped his notebook with the back of

his hand. "That's the stuff," he said. "I think we've got it."

"Yes," said Smashie. "And tomorrow we will tax both John and Billy with the crime and see who cracks first!"

Dontel beamed.

"I love when we call questioning people about things 'taxing them with their crimes.' We do like that part," he said.

"Yes," said Smashie. "We do."

"Although," said Dontel thoughtfully, "taxing people doesn't always go so well for us."

Smashie wilted a little. "That is true." But then she squared her shoulders. "But I have a good feeling about it this time. My money's on John. I've never seen him so against something in my whole life, and we've been in the same class since kindergarten."

"I agree," said Dontel. "But we have to keep an open mind. All of our suspects are just that: suspects. Innocent until proven guilty."

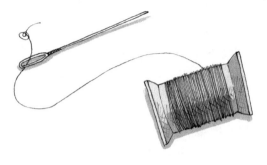

CHAPTER 13

Taxing!

That evening, Smashie worked on her new Investigator Suit. She consulted her mother.

"What about the Choreographer Suit we were
working on?" asked Mrs. McPerter, somewhat startled.

"I need that, too," said Smashie. "But for tomorrow, I want something that makes me look ready for
justice."

"Why do you need to look ready for justice?" asked
her mother.

"I just do," said Smashie.

"Hmm," said Mrs. McPerter. "This isn't going to be like that Patches suit, is it? Because I remember a lot of hectic fallout from that one."

"No," Smashie said. "I just like justice."

"Well, how about that old blue satin jacket I had in high school?" her mother offered. "That could kind of look like something an officer of the law would wear."

"Great idea!" said Smashie. And although the jacket reached to her knees, it gave her the perfect investigator feeling she had been hoping for.

"I was going to try to find a flat cap," she confided to Dontel at their cubbies the next morning. "But I thought that might be too police-looking and put people on guard again."

And she took off her hoodie and placed it in her cubby. Over the satin jacket, Smashie had wrapped a tool belt belonging to her grandmother around her waist. She'd had to wrap it around twice, but it worked pretty okay. Her jeans were just jeans, but she thought they rounded out the blue of the jacket nicely.

"More like a policewoman," she whispered to Dontel. "And I put lots of pockets for clues on the belt, just in case. With room for my notebook in one of the pouches."

Dontel nodded tactfully.

"Now," said Smashie, "let's get to taxing." But her relief was short-lived.

"Smashie," called Ms. Early, "is that a suit?"

The double-wrapped tool belt made the jacket press uncomfortably into Smashie's middle. "Sort of," she said.

"It's not some kind of disruptive suit, is it?" asked Ms. Early, her tone light but her eyes sharp. "One that might distract the class?"

"No," said Smashie uncertainly. "It's . . . it's to help with the musicale." It was technically true, but Smashie squirmed.

"Oh!" Ms. Early smiled. "Is it a Choreographer Suit?"

But before Smashie had time to answer, there was an interruption. Joyce appeared in the doorway. Her normally shy face was unhappy. And she was furious.

"You said your mom could do hair!" she shouted at Charlene. The rest of Room 11 tilted their heads to one side, staring at Joyce.

"Hmm," said Siggie.

"It looks kind of like a hedge," said Alonso.

"More like one of those bonsai trees Mr. Bloom clips into shapes in his storage room," said Cyrus.

"*Ugh!*" cried Joyce. "All I wanted was a haircut!"

"In a good way, it looks like those things," said Smashie hastily. She knew how it was to have an unruly head of hair. But she had to admit that even hers had never looked quite as terrible as Joyce's did now. Still,

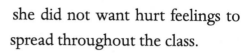

she did not want hurt feelings to spread throughout the class.

"My hair heart looked so nice that my mother wanted to support Charlene's mom and our class by bringing me to her for a haircut after my orthodontist appointment yesterday! She bought our class a jar of goop at the same time so we wouldn't have to use our planetarium money," Joyce explained. "And now look at me! My hair looks like a group of potatoes! Charlene, you are one of my best friends, and I want to support you, BUT YOUR MOM WRECKED MY HEAD!"

Joyce was near tears.

"You can borrow my balaclava helmet," Alonso offered Joyce.

Charlene's eyes brimmed, too. "My mom hasn't really cut hair in a while," she said with a gulp, "after doing sculpture at the salon where she used to work for so long. She's kind of rusty. I'm sorry, Joyce! We will fix your hair for free!"

Joyce handed her the jar of goop. "Goop me up

again instead, please," she said. "As nice as yesterday's hair heart. Nice enough to make me and my mom feel better about my wrecked-up hair."

"And the rest of you, think long and hard before you go over there," said Billy.

"Billy!" said Ms. Early sternly.

"None of us was really planning to," said John.

But Charlene was already palming the goop onto Joyce's hair. And there, poking up from Joyce's head, were two darling little ponytails in the shape of roller-skate wheels. "Because you're in the roller-skating number, too," Charlene said.

"Hmm," said Joyce. "Mirror."

Siggie passed one over.

After a long moment, Joyce spoke. "Charlene, you are lucky that you have inherited your mom's skill with hair sculpting." She beamed, all thought of tears forgotten. "I'm adorable!"

"You are!"

"For real!"

"Charlene, we won't doubt you again!"

"Speak for yourself," John muttered. "I don't think any amount of sculpture makes up for getting a crazy haircut."

The class fell silent. Charlene's eyes grew troubled once more.

"Charlene," said Ms. Early, "don't you worry. We'll support your mother and help her get her business on its feet." She put her arm around the sad-faced girl. "I know you're anxious." And she drew Charlene to one side to talk. Jacinda watched her friend with concerned eyes.

Smashie and Dontel looked at each other. It was time for taxing.

Glancing at the front of the room where Ms. Early was still speaking to Charlene, they turned to John. "So. You don't want us to do it?"

"Do what?" John asked. "Get people's heads mangled with awful haircuts?"

"No," said Smashie. "The musicale."

John cast his eyes down. "No," he said. "I don't."

Smashie and Dontel looked at each other in triumph. An abashed John admitting he didn't want Room 11 to do the musicale could only mean one thing! He wanted to shut the whole thing down. With a vengeance!

But they were wrong.

"But my dad says to face my fear," said John. "And I'm going to. No musicale is going to lick me."

He got up from his seat and moved to the front of the room. He tapped Ms. Early on the shoulder.

"I'm sorry for how I've been acting," he told her. "And I want to do a number. I want to sing a song called 'Come On Over to My Place.'"

Dontel and Smashie were shocked into motionlessness.

"By Hyacinth Rooney?" exclaimed Ms. Early, her arm still around Charlene. "She's one of my favorites! Do you have a backup track you can use?"

"No," said John grimly. "I'll accompany myself. On the piano."

The class applauded. Smashie and Dontel looked at each other.

"I am proud of you, John," said Ms. Early. "Very. And I am proud of Charlene as well for trying so hard to help with our Hair Extravaganza and Musicale."

She walked Charlene back to her seat. "Now, let's get to work on our math again. We have some new ideas to explore."

"We may like taxing people," whispered Dontel, "but it doesn't always go so well."

"We barely even got to tax him!" Smashie whispered back, crestfallen. "Our best suspect—gone!"

Smashie's tool belt came loose and clattered to the ground.

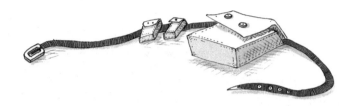

CHAPTER 14

Mystery in Math Class

Ms. Early met her eye. "Smashie," she said, "you assured me that suit would not be disruptive."

"Sorry, Ms. Early," said Smashie, and fixed her belt. She sat with her cheeks in her hands. So far, this new Investigator Suit was not doing the trick. And now Ms. Early was irritated with her, too. How was that going to put her in a frame of mind to let Smashie sing in the musicale? Smashie had better watch her step, was what.

"I'd like to look at that problem I gave you for homework," said Ms. Early. "How many tens in two hundred and fifty-nine?"

But Dontel and Smashie, who normally adored math class, were both distracted and could scarcely pay attention.

"Sort yourselves into groups of four or five and compare your work," said Ms. Early. "I want all of you to really *think*, Room 11."

Dontel shook his head wearily at Smashie. "We might as well try taxing Billy now," he said.

Smashie pulled her mind back to the investigation. "Even though we are the world's worst taxers today," she agreed.

"Dontel and Smashie," called Ms. Early, "are you paying attention?"

"Yes," said Dontel. "I was just going to ask Billy to work with me and Smashie."

"Sure," said Billy.

"Can I, too?" asked Cyrus.

"And me?" asked Jacinda.

"That'd be great," said Smashie. But in her heart

she despaired. Losing John as a suspect was a giant failure. She had been so sure he was the perp! Billy was a pale second choice. And how were they going to tax him anyhow, in front of Cyrus and Jacinda?

But she grabbed a bin of math cubes and a sheaf of paper and headed with Billy and Dontel to the meeting area rug to work. As they passed Ms. Early's desk, Smashie began to hum a few bars of "Smacked in the Heart."

But "Be sparing with that paper, Smashie" was all Ms. Early said. "We are running low."

Smashie's heart sank. "We will be," she said, and slouched back over to her group.

Dontel looked at her. She shook her head. He patted her comfortingly on the arm.

"What's the suit, Smash?" Jacinda asked amiably, joining them from the back of the room, a pencil in her hand.

"Oh, just a . . . just a suit," said Smashie. "For . . . for choreographing. And thinking," she said, still unhappy with her attempt with Ms. Early but uncomfortable with her fib. "So how many tens do you all think we can make out of that number?" she asked her group.

But the other children were still eyeing Smashie's suit.

"My mom and dad have belts like that," said Cyrus. "They're mechanics, so they always have tools handy."

"My dad works with computers, but he got laid off a while ago," said Jacinda. "He's still looking for a job. But my mom's a patent lawyer."

"What's a patent lawyer?"

"They help you make sure no one else can copy an idea you have for an invention or something."

"Oh," said Smashie. "Well, my mom's a phlebotomist. They're the ones that take your blood at the doctor."

"Ugh!" said Jacinda. "I hate needles!"

"Everybody does," said Smashie. "My mom says it's tough being the one no one wants to see."

"Smashie's group! Get to work!" Ms. Early was stern.

The group hastily started working.

Smashie wrote in large numerals at the top of a piece of paper.

"Here, Smashie," said Billy. "Have some cubes. Let's see how many tens we can use to build this."

"Thanks," said Smashie. She glanced over in Ms. Early's direction. Ms. Early was busy with Tatiana's group and was not looking their way. "Bet you're still real mad about the musicale, huh?" she said, arranging cubes into sticks of ten. "Because you can't sing 'Machine Gun Jailbreak'?"

"'Machine Gun Jailbreak' is a great song," said Billy determinedly.

"Billy," said Smashie meaningfully.

"Oh, heck, I don't care if I can't sing it," said Billy. Smashie dropped her cubes.

"I knew Ms. Early wouldn't let me sing 'Machine Gun Jailbreak,'" Billy continued. "I was just stirring things up. And besides, all I really want is my hair lengthened and molded into a shape. I can't wait for the musicale!"

Dontel looked up from his own work, shocked. "What?" he said incredulously.

"Yeah," said Billy happily. "A good hair molding will be a blast. My mom'll freak. I'm hoping Charlene can make me an actual hair roller-skate shape like Tatiana's! Or if I don't have enough hair for that"—his eyes glinted—"maybe she can mold me into some kind of monster! And I can tell my mom it's permanent!"

Smashie and Dontel looked at each other in despair. Both their suspects had fended them off before they could even tax them—and fended them off spectacularly. The motives they had thought of yesterday had completely fallen apart. Neither John nor Billy had any desire at all to sabotage the musicale. And it was clear that Billy actively wanted Charlene to use the goop on him, so it was no prank of his, either.

Ugh!

They had no more suspects. Smashie's suit had failed and so had all the notions sparked by yesterday's motion, including Dontel's plan to convince Ms. Early to let Smashie sing. What were they going to do?

"Ms. Early!" Joyce was at her cubby. "I just came back here to get some markers from my backpack, and guess what!"

Smashie and Dontel sat up straight, their failures forgotten.

"The hair goop is gone!" cried Dontel before Ms. Early could respond.

"Yes!" cried Joyce. "How did you know? What is going on in here?"

CHAPTER 15

A Devastating Suspect

Once again, Room 11 exploded in talk.

"That's the third missing jar!" cried Siggie.

"It is!" wailed Willette. "Why is all our goop going missing?"

"It certainly is strange," said Ms. Early, frowning a bit.

"Everything in our room goes missing!" cried Tatiana. "First our hamster, now our goop!"

"We can't do our Hair Extravaganza and Musicale

without our special hair!" cried Joyce. "We're going to have to cancel!"

John stared at her, his gaze torn somewhere between disappointment and hope. Charlene's eyes were like saucers.

"Pool our resources!" Smashie shouted, one fist raised. "Everybody has to bring in what smells good from their house! Like vanilla and fancy soaps you use only for guests! Charlene can help us invent hair goop for ourselves in science class!"

"Now, don't everybody get all worked up," said Ms. Early. "Smashie, especially you."

"What do you mean?" cried Smashie, stung. But she knew. She rather liked to get worked up, and Ms. Early often had to calm her down. Especially during the hamster episode.

"Wait a minute," said Dontel. "I smell lavender. Do you?"

The class lifted its collective noses skyward, sniffing.

"I do," said John, "but why wouldn't we? Joyce is covered in the stuff."

"It's on my hands, too," Charlene pointed out.

"But I could swear . . ." Dontel's voice trailed off.

"Class." Ms. Early was firm. "We are not going to make more of this than is rational." She glanced at the clock above the open door to the classroom. "I think that does it for math. We certainly didn't get very far. Put your things away, children, and get ready for recess."

The rumble of Mr. Bloom's cleaning cart passed by their door. Smashie stared. For behind the cart was Mr. Bloom.

His hair was lengthened. And molded. Into something of a shape.

"He looked like Ben Franklin!" Smashie told Dontel on the blacktop once the class arrived out of doors for morning recess. "Mr. Bloom usually just has a rim of hair around his bald spot. But today he has LENGTHENED AND MOLDED locks flowing around his bald spot, just like our country's famous forefather!"

"Mr. Bloom?" Dontel was incredulous. "But that makes no sense!" He whipped out his Investigation Notebook and turned to the Opportunity List. "Wait a minute. Maybe it does."

"What do you mean?" asked Smashie.

"Well, he came in our room after the second jar went missing. With the recycling bins, remember?"

Smashie shuddered. Of course she remembered, what with Mrs. Armstrong coming to shout at her at the same time. "But he wasn't in our room at all during math today. And that's when the jar of goop Joyce brought in went missing. Do you think maybe he is getting one of the kids to steal it for him?" said Smashie.

"Smashie!" said Dontel. "I can't imagine that Mr. Bloom—one of our favorite adults—would ask one of us kids to *steal*! That's just nuts!"

"I don't know, Dontel! All I know is that he is the only person with lengthened and molded hair that didn't get it done by Charlene in our class!"

"It does explain why I smelled that lavender and lilac even more," said Dontel reluctantly. "If he was passing by our door."

"Yes," said Smashie. "And since he was in the hallway earlier, too. That's a clue! We should add that to the list."

And, very hastily, she took out her Investigation Notebook from her tool belt and wrote:

> The thief probably smells like the goop
> because that is a super strong smell
> that sticks with you.

"Maybe it's a conspiracy of all the baldish teachers!" Smashie cried. "Maybe Mr. Flange will be next!" While Mr. Flange, the art teacher, had a luxurious mustache, it was true that he had barely a spear of hair left on his head. "If Mr. Flange shows up tomorrow with hair in a wild hairdo, then we'll know! We can tax *all* the unhairy teachers! We can—"

"Smashie," said Dontel, "I think we have to calm down. We need a plan."

"Well, I know what our next plan is," said Smashie firmly. "Tax Mr. Bloom."

"It just feels wrong to me," said Dontel. "I can't help it. He's so nice about talking to me about space. I don't want to disrespect him!"

"I know." Smashie's hectic thoughts slowed. "I really like him, too. But you are the one who said we couldn't let personal feelings get in the way. If Mr. Bloom is a thief, he must be brought to justice. We are good at that. Better than at taxing people, even."

"True," said Dontel. He thought for a moment. Then he sighed. "All right. Fine. Ms. Early said our room is low on paper. We could ask Miss Martone, the yard lady, if we could go to Mr. Bloom's trailer to get paper and then talk to him while we're there."

"All right," Smashie agreed, "but I don't think that lady likes me much still. After yesterday and the Jerk and all."

"Let me do the talking," said Dontel.

They made their way toward the yard lady, passing Jacinda and Charlene, who were, as yesterday, watching Carlos from Room 12 across the blacktop. Carlos's shoulders looked hunchy, like he knew Charlene's eyes were upon him.

"This whole like-like thing is weird," said Smashie.

"Tell me about it," said Dontel.

"What do you two want?" asked Miss Martone as they reached her. "Here to call me a jerk again?"

"We're real sorry you thought that, ma'am," said Dontel. "Smashie here feels terrible."

Smashie nodded.

"The dance isn't called the Jerk like an insult," Dontel explained. "It means jerk like jerk your arms around. Smashie here was just teaching the kids. For our musicale."

"Oh," said the yard lady. "Well! That does make more sense." And she smiled at Smashie and Dontel. "I get it now. No hard feelings." And she rumpled Smashie's hair. Smashie didn't mind. Now that her hair music note had been washed out, it was already pretty sticky-outy again.

"We were just going to ask you if we can go get some more paper for our room from Mr. Bloom," said Dontel. "We're low."

"Sure thing," said Miss Martone. "Just don't miss the whistle at the end of recess."

"We won't," said Dontel, and off they went.

CHAPTER 16

Terrible Taxing

Normally, Smashie and Dontel loved to go visit Mr. Bloom in his little trailer just outside the main building. All of the children at the Rebecca Lee Crumpler Elementary School did. Besides being filled with supplies for the classrooms and for cleaning, it was full of Mr. Bloom's hobbies as well: tiny bonsai trees he had pruned into beautiful shapes and lots of reading material about alien life-forms. And his music player bellowed opera songs through the open windows and doors of the trailer all day long. But Smashie and

Dontel were not happy at all as they made their way to the trailer with their dark, sad suspicions about the man who had always been one of their favorite adults in the school.

"This is our worst case ever," said Smashie. "Why do we have to keep suspecting our friends?"

"It is only our second case, Smashie," Dontel pointed out. "But you are right about the part about our friends."

"*Mi chiamano Mimì, ma il mio nome è Lucia . . .*" A lady sang Italianly from the trailer as they approached.

Through the open door, Mr. Bloom was working his hands over his hair. And before their very eyes, his hair transformed from the Ben Franklin hanks Smashie had described to Dontel to something more like the aging rock stars on the albums Smashie's mother loved to play.

Mr. Bloom heard them and turned around. "Why, hello there, Miss McP. and Mr. M.! Nice to see you! What can I do you for?"

The scent of lavender was overpowering.

"We need . . . paper," said Dontel faintly.

"Coming right up. Let me just wash this goop off

my hands. Wonderful stuff. 'Course you two are too young to worry about hair loss, but, my stars, this is doing the trick! Until I wash it, I guess. Herr Goop, it's called. Heh, heh! Pretty clever, that. It says right on the jar that it lengthens and molds the hair, and darned if it doesn't! Check me out!"

"It looks super," Smashie said uncomfortably. She and Dontel looked at each other in shock. Was Mr. Bloom confessing to stealing right before their eyes? But why didn't he seem sorry? Or ashamed? Or ready to turn himself in to the authorities? Maybe Mr. Bloom was such a hardened criminal that he didn't even care if he was discovered! Maybe he *rejoiced* in the revelation of his crimes!

Be brave, Smashie, Smashie said to herself. *Start taxing him!*

"Mr. Bloom," she said in a strangled voice, "when did you get that goop?"

Mr. Bloom finished washing his hands and moved to the large boxes of ruled paper he kept near his bonsai trees. "Oh, just a couple of days ago. I believe it was the day you folks planned your big musicale.

Which I'm very much looking forward to, by the by. I love a good musical number."

And he whistled along to the Italian lady as if he hadn't a care in the world.

"May I see the jar?" asked Dontel.

"Sure." Mr. Bloom tossed it to him and, still whistling, headed over to extract several reams of paper from a box. Exactly like a proud stealie-pants would!

"This jar is the one, all right," whispered Dontel to Smashie. "The first one Charlene used on you."

Smashie looked at it and agreed. There hadn't been serial numbers on that first jar, and there were none on this one, either. Clearly this was made before Charlene's mom got the idea to use those numbers to label their product.

Dontel handed the jar back to Mr. Bloom as the custodian placed the paper carefully into their befuddled, suspicious arms.

"Mr. Bloom," said Smashie, gulping, "what about the other jars? When did you take those?"

Mr. Bloom looked puzzled. "Well, I'd say I 'found' that jar, rather than 'took' it, Miss McP."

"Found?" said Dontel.

"It was in the hallway right outside Room 11 — your room."

"But what about the other jars?"

"*Other* jars?" said Mr. Bloom. "What other jars? This is the only jar I found. I didn't take other jars. Heck, all I did was find this one, and it gave me real hope."

"But two more went missing from our room, too!" said Smashie, studying Mr. Bloom's face for signs of pride in his thievery.

"And you came in with the recycling bins when one of them—" Dontel began bravely.

"What?" Mr. Bloom cut him off. "You kids came in here thinking I *stole* the goop from your class?" His feelings were clearly hurt.

Dontel swallowed. "It's just that the jars keep going missing."

Mr. Bloom's eyes widened. "Well, I only found the one, and here"—he handed it to Smashie—"you take it back right now. I've used a lot of it, but I sure didn't mean to take your supply. I thought it was just something that had been tossed away. And I certainly didn't *take* any others." His shoulders slumped and he shook his head. "Never thought I'd see the day when two decent kids like yourselves would accuse me of thieving. I surely did not."

Smashie felt terrible. Of course Mr. Bloom was not a stealie-pants! Why had she ever even thought it?

"We're sorry, Mr. Bloom!" cried Smashie.

"It must have rolled out the door like Ms. Early said," said Dontel, bowing his head in shame.

"You keep that goop," said Smashie. "Please! Your hair looks great!"

"I can't do that," said Mr. Bloom. "Not with you kids thinking so poorly of me. Not if it's going to make everybody in Room 11 think I'm a thief." He sighed. "It's too bad. I did promise Mr. Flange he could have a go."

Smashie's mind filled with the image of their taciturn art teacher sporting a lengthened and molded mustache.

"Please keep it," Dontel begged the custodian. "Please. We're sorry we taxed you. We know you'd never do anything dishonest. And our class doesn't even know about what we thought."

Mr. Bloom hesitated, then took the jar from

Smashie. "Well, if you say so. I sure hope you find your missing goop."

"We do, too," said Smashie.

But Mr. Bloom's shoulders were still sagging as Smashie and Dontel left the trailer, their arms full of paper and hearts full of guilt.

"We are awful, awful children," said Smashie as they made their way back to the blacktop. Recess was almost over, and the rest of the third-graders were already lining up to go in.

"I know," said Dontel miserably. "And terrible investigators, too. We haven't picked a single suspect that has even turned out to be for-real suspicious!"

"And we are still goopless because we gave Mr. Bloom back the goop he had. You know what this means, Dontel?"

"Kids will drop out of the Hair Extravaganza and Musicale because of no cool hair," said Dontel unhappily. "And our teacher will be very sad."

Hrmm, thought Smashie. "Well, I have to admit I do think it would help if you would at least wear an Investigator Suit, too, while we work on this case."

"I don't need an old suit," said Dontel. "I keep

what I need in my pockets." This was true. Dontel's pockets were always a treasure trove of things he found that might come in handy. Right now, his front pockets contained six pistachios, two springs that had sprung out of a ballpoint pen, and a tiny two-by-one-inch pocket dictionary. In his back pocket was his Investigation Notebook.

"What do you mean, *an old suit?*" Smashie cried. "I thought you understood about suits!"

"I do," said Dontel. "I'm sorry, Smash. Let's not fight. What we need to do," he said, "is more investigating."

"Yes," said Smashie. "And find a way to apologize to Mr. Bloom." She drooped under the weight of the paper and her troubles. No sooner had Smashie

straightened things out with the yard lady than she had messed things up with another adult. And they were no closer to finding out who had taken the missing hair goop and why.

Overhead the sun disappeared behind the clouds. A rumble of thunder rolled across the play yard as the whistle blew.

The rumble of thunder turned to rain almost as soon as Room 11 came indoors, and Smashie and Dontel handed the heavy reams of paper to Ms. Early.

"Why, thank you!" Ms. Early was delighted. "You've saved me an errand."

"You're welcome," said Dontel, but Smashie could tell he was still feeling as down as she was.

"Saved Ms. Early an errand," whispered Smashie, "but now Mr. Bloom will never be our friend again." She squirmed under the weight of her suit's tool belt. "And forget about me humming around Ms. Early again. Once she finds out we accused Mr. Bloom, she'll never let me sing!"

"I'm afraid you're right," said Dontel sadly. "And Mr. Bloom and I were going to talk about rockets next week. But I bet we won't, now."

CHAPTER 17

Worry in Room 11

"Come to the meeting area, please, children," said Ms. Early the next morning. "It's time for us to finalize our list of acts, because guess what! We're going to start rehearsing with both classes tomorrow! I've reserved the auditorium after lunch for us to work on some of the musical numbers, and Miss Dismont will take everybody else into the gym to work with Smashie and Dontel on our interludes. Smashie and Dontel, have you and your grammy and dad finalized the dances?"

"Yes," said Smashie, glad to have something positive to contribute for once. She was still wearing her Investigator Suit from yesterday. "For the most part. May I write them on the chart?"

"Certainly," said Ms. Early, and handed Smashie a marker.

"We tried to match the dances to the acts as much as we could," explained Dontel. "Just like Charlene is doing with our hair."

"If we ever find our goop again," said Joyce, touching her roller-skate ponytails. Clearly she was worried about how she would look after they had been washed out. Room 11 buzzed again as the children considered the implications of the missing goop.

"If I get my hands on that thief —" said Cyrus.

"Never mind that," said someone else. "If there's no goop, why bother doing the musicale at all?"

"Enough," said Ms. Early, though Smashie could tell she was concerned as well. "Smashie, why don't you print the names of the dances in the spots on the chart now?"

"All right," said Smashie.

THIRD-GRADE HAIR EXTRAVAGANZA AND MUSICALE

1. Opening dance to get everyone peppy: THE PONY

2. Siggie alphabetizes with backup singers

3. Dance: THE SWIM

4. Alonso and Lilia sing duet of "Endless Amour"
with backup singers

5. Dance: THE TEMPTATION WALK

6. Dontel speaks a piece about astronomy
and the cosmos

7. Dance:

Smashie paused here.

"We haven't decided on a dance for after my piece,"
said Dontel. "The Jerk has the best arm motions to
represent the movement of parts of the universe, but
we promised Mrs. Armstrong we wouldn't do that
one."

"We certainly did," said Ms. Early, "and I'm afraid
I'm holding us to it."

"We'll figure out another dance," said Smashie.

8. Tatiana sings "Roll Roll Roll Your Roller Skates"
with backup singers

9. Dance: THE SKATE

10. John sings and plays "Come On Over to My Place"

11. Finale Dance: THE MASHED POTATO!

Tatiana looked pleased but puzzled.

"Which dances match the acts besides the Skate with my song? Thank you for that, by the way."

"You're welcome," said Dontel. "Well, we also thought the Mashed Potato matched John's number—"

John groaned. "Don't remind me. My neck!"

"Be strong," said Cyrus. "You can do it."

"My grammy looked up the lyrics," said Smashie, "and the lady in the song talks about a lot of food she's going to give the person who comes on over to her place. There was so much we figured she'd probably give the person mashed potatoes, too, John."

"I can see that, actually," said John. "Sorry. I guess I'm still pretty nervous."

"We understand," said Dontel.

"And the Swim seems like the way alphabetizing feels," said Smashie.

There was a silence.

"What?" asked Room 11 as a body.

"Well, you know how it feels like you are swimming through all those letters and working so hard to keep everything straight?"

There was another silence.

"I guess I am the only one who feels that way," said Smashie, crestfallen. "But it really is a fun dance."

"It sounds like it," said Siggie. "And it will be neat to see what Charlene can do with our hair for that one."

"If we ever get our goop back," said Joyce sadly.

"If we don't get it back . . ." A voice trailed away. But Smashie and Dontel knew what that meant. Another member of Room 11 on the verge of dropping out of the musicale. They needed to find the goop thief, and fast, before more kids fell back to the same idea. Smashie's heart began to pound with worry.

But she continued explaining the dances. "My grammy says the Temptation Walk will be good with 'Endless Amour,'" she said.

"That is going to be a lot of hairstyles to do for eleven numbers," Cyrus observed. "How can we do it with no goop?"

"There is plenty of time to worry about that," said Ms. Early. "If worse comes to worst, I'm sure Charlene can style your hair in some other way, without it."

But Smashie could tell that Ms. Early was worried.

"Well, no goop, no me," said someone at the back of the room.

"Hey!" said Smashie. "Who said that? Aren't we all in this together, even without interesting hair?"

"Yeah!" cried the part of Room 11 committed to the musicale for reasons not to do with hair. But enough voices remained silent that Ms. Early drew herself up. "The list of acts is marvelous. We will proceed as planned. Now, let's get to our math."

Ms. Early uncapped a dry-erase marker and began to write on the whiteboard. "I'd like all of you to think about what Siggie shared yesterday about using the numbers of tens in each hundred of a number in order to make a three-digit number using as many tens as possible."

But Smashie's mind was still too awhirl with their incomplete investigation to pay her usual close attention to math as Ms. Early handed the marker to Siggie and he wrote his thinking on the board.

Who would take the other jars of goop? And why? What are the chances of both the other jars having rolled away as well? No. It had to be a member of Room 11. And she and Dontel had to get back to work, investigating, before people started dropping out of the musicale like flies.

Dontel was clearly having a similar group of thoughts. "It'll be an indoor lunch recess in the gym because of the rain," he said. "We'll sit somewhere away from the others and get back to the drawing board, investigation-wise."

"And we better think of a way to make it up to Mr. Bloom as well," said Smashie sadly.

"Yes," said Dontel. "I am going to dedicate my astronomy speech to him."

"That's great!" said Smashie. "But that won't be for another six days. I don't want him to be upset with us for six more days!"

"And what if the other kids find out?" said Dontel. "Everybody will be awful mad."

"Ugh," said Smashie. It was true. "That would make three problems for us to solve."

"Three?" asked Dontel. "Finding the goop and

getting the kids to stay in the musicale—that's two." He looked at Smashie. "Oh, yes. And getting Ms. Early to let you sing."

But Smashie's shoulders drooped. She was already so embarrassed about her failures in this regard and all of her rumpled-up feelings about Ms. Early that she didn't want to talk about her own problem again right now. "Besides," she said, finishing her thought aloud, "we better unravel the goop one as soon as possible! The whole success of our Hair Extravaganza and Musicale is at stake!" And that was more important than her singing and feeling comfortable around Ms. Early.

Wasn't it?

CHAPTER 18

Found Out

When they arrived at the gym for indoor recess, Miss Martone was there with her whistle, helping kids organize games. Smashie and Dontel headed to the other end of the gym, hoping to find a hidden corner to work in.

"It's awfully loud in here," said Dontel. "Not the best for thinking."

"A good investigator works under even the worst circumstances," said Smashie firmly. "Let's sit next to the basketball bins. We can lean our backs against the wall. It's a little more private that way."

"Yes," Dontel agreed. "And maybe the bins will dam up some of the noise."

"I think we should think of other kinds of motives," said Smashie as they settled into their spot. She prised her Investigation Notebook out of its tool-belt spot and opened up to the Motives List.

Dontel nodded. "Yep," he said. "We better cross out the one about wanting to lengthen and mold hair. I mean, it turned out that's why Mr. Bloom kept the jar, but not because he is a thief."

Both of them turned bleak eyes toward the gym's double doorways, where Mr. Bloom and his rock-star hair stood talking with the yard lady.

"But the second and third jars," said Smashie. "There has to be a motive for taking those. It's too much of a coincidence to think they rolled away, too, isn't it?"

"I thought so at first," said Dontel. "But maybe it isn't."

"But the jars were in class. We saw them. The jars would have to have taken magical leaps to get out of Room 11 unaided. Dontel! Maybe that's it! Maybe the jars are turbocharged! You know about rockets—maybe Charlene's mother is a secret rocket inventor and she is testing her ideas on the hair goop jars! Maybe—"

"Smashie," said Dontel, "you're getting carried away. I think it is probably more logical that someone took the jars."

Smashie was deflated. Her idea was much more fun. But she had to admit that Dontel had a point. "Oh, fine," she said. "Let's write that down."

"What are you guys doing?"

Smashie jumped. It was Joyce, Cyrus, Charlene, and Siggie.

"Oh, we're . . . we're just trying to think of a new dance to match my astronomy speech," said Dontel. Smashie looked at him in surprise at the quickness of his excuse.

A red ball careered toward them from the other side of the room. It bounced off the wall right over Smashie's and Dontel's heads. Cyrus caught it on the rebound.

"Hey!" Smashie cried.

Carlos and several other kids from Room 12 ran toward them. "I'm sorry!" cried Carlos. "It was my fault! We're playing keep-away and I passed in the wrong direction!" He caught sight of Charlene and gulped. She stared at him.

"Take a picture, you two—it'll last longer," muttered Cyrus.

"It's okay, Carlos," said Dontel. "Whew, though. You almost clocked us."

"We'll be real careful for the rest of the game," promised Carlos.

"Indoor recess is never as much fun as playing outside," said Charlene. "Let's all go play keep-away."

"Keep-away!" Smashie shuddered. All those balls

pelting around and having to try to catch them. Bluck!

"Oh, come on, Smashie! It's fun!" Charlene pleaded.

"Just you make sure you put those balls away after. You kids give me quite a time finding them when you forget."

It was Mr. Bloom.

"Hi, Mr. Bloom!" cried the standing children. Smashie and Dontel looked down, ashamed. "We'll tidy up! Promise!"

"Me and Smashie can do it," said Dontel, looking up hopefully at Mr. Bloom. "We want to help, too."

Mr. Bloom shook his head. "I suppose you two think I'll lift a couple to take home," he said sadly. "Thanks, kids, for cleaning up." And he moved off toward the gym doors.

"What did he mean by that?" Siggie wondered aloud.

Smashie squirmed. "We . . . we kind of thought maybe he was responsible for the missing hair goop. On account of his hair looking so lush."

Cyrus was indignant. "Did you *accuse* Mr. Bloom?" he squawked.

Dontel gulped. "Kind of."

Smashie blushed. "A little bit. We did. But it turned out he just found it. It had rolled away. He used it, but he didn't steal it."

"I can't believe you ever thought he did!" cried Cyrus. "Mr. Bloom is the nicest adult in this school!"

"Yes!" said Joyce. "How could you?"

"We didn't mean—"

"We apologized—"

"So that *is* an Investigator Suit!" cried Charlene. "I thought so, but it was different from your Patches one so I didn't say."

Smashie looked down miserably at her satin jacket.

"Yes," she said. "It is."

"You two better stop investigating right now and quit accusing nice people the whole time!" said Charlene.

"Yeah!" said Jacinda. "You should quit it right now!"

"Come on," said Siggie. "Let's forget these two and go play keep-away."

"You two just sit here and think," said Joyce. "Maybe you'll come up with something else to make Mr. Bloom feel terrible about."

"Better move out of the way, though," said Charlene. "Who knows where our keep-away ball might end up again?"

And the children ran off with Carlos and his friends, Charlene looking back at them and scowling.

Smashie and Dontel hung their heads.

CHAPTER 19

A Discovery

"This," said Smashie, "is extremely terrible."

"Yes," said Dontel. "It is. But we can't stop investigating. If Charlene weren't so mad at us, she would say that, too! That goop is as essential to our musicale as it is to her mom's new business! We need to find out who's taking it and get it back."

"And we can't even apologize to Mr. Bloom again because he's already gone," said Smashie. "Not to mention all of Room 11 being upset with us for hurting his feelings."

"It's not everyone," Dontel pointed out. "Just the four of them. And a few Room 12 kids."

"It'll be all of them by the time recess is over," said Smashie. And she was right. Already, they could see Joyce and Charlene whispering to the other children playing keep-away. Everybody was stealing looks in Smashie and Dontel's direction.

"Should we just give up the investigation like the kids said?" said Dontel.

Smashie looked at him, startled. Usually she was the one who wanted recklessly to give up, and Dontel was the one who steadied her through, but now she mustered herself to support her friend. "No," she said. "There is wrongdoing afoot, Dontel! I keep telling you, investigators have to persist. Remember how bad it got in the Patches investigation? But we stuck with it anyway!"

It was true. The Patches investigation had had some truly trying moments.

"I do," said Dontel. He drew himself up. "All right. Thanks for talking sense into me, Smash."

"No problem."

"And you're right that something is afoot. . . . I just

know something is up. I have this feeling. . . ." His voice trailed off. "But I don't know why I have it," he confessed.

"It will come to you," Smashie reassured Dontel. "But we have to press on. Let's get back to more motives."

"Maybe someone doesn't like Charlene and wants her not to be able to do the hairstyles?"

"You mean, like they are maybe jealous of her talent? And the attention she's getting?"

"Could be," said Dontel. "Let's put that down."

5. People are jealous of or don't like Charlene.

"I don't know who, though," said Dontel. "Everybody loved Joyce's hair heart and roller-skate wheels, and you loved your hairdo, too."

"True. And everyone just seems excited to get one of those hairdos, not jealous that Charlene could do them. And it does seem like Joyce has forgiven Charlene for her bad haircut. They sat together at lunch," Smashie said.

Across the room the red rubber balls were

bouncing, and children were shouting and laughing. A few stole looks at Smashie and Dontel from time to time. Smashie's neck felt hot.

Dontel sighed. "I guess the kids really are all fans of the goop. And Charlene."

Across the gym, Jacinda ran like a gazelle, passing the ball to Cyrus.

"I am losing hope," said Smashie. "I wish I had paid more attention to the jars when we saw them."

"I did pay attention," said Dontel absently. Across the room, Charlene passed the ball to Siggie. Carlos intercepted it but dropped it when he caught sight of Charlene.

"*We win!*" Charlene screamed.

"At least someone in our class is happy, even if just for now," said Smashie. "Man. Between Mr. Bloom and my not getting my math done today—" She broke off. Dontel was not listening. His eyes were glued to the base of the basketball bin.

"What are you staring at?" asked Smashie.

"Smashie," said Dontel in a strangled voice, "I have just found a clue!"

CHAPTER 20

The Key
to the
Case

"A clue!" cried Smashie. Luckily her shout was drowned out by the din of the playing children.

"Yes," said Dontel. And he reached behind one of the rear wheels of the basketball bin and brought out a jar. A familiar-looking jar.

"That's not just a clue! That's the stolen goods itself!" cried Smashie. "What? Who? How?"

"I don't know," said Dontel. "But now I *know* we're onto something. I've remembered what made me think so before!"

But before he could go on, the *PHWEET* of the yard lady's whistle sounded and it was time to line up.

Dontel placed the jar carefully back where he found it.

"Why are you putting it back?" Smashie was plaintive. "We need to show the kids! We can be heroes! We can do some hairstyles after all! And now maybe the rest of them will forgive us for Mr. Bloom! Take the jar!"

"No," said Dontel. "I've got good reasons. Trust me, Smash."

And although she was full of misgivings, Smashie nodded. Dontel was the finest thinker she knew. She did trust him. But it was certainly hard to control her patience. And it was even harder to join a line of children who were all mad at them. The frostiness toward Smashie and Dontel was palpable.

"Didn't see you doing much dancing," said Cyrus to them as they walked down the hall. "What, were you too busy thinking of other people to accuse?"

"We said we were sorry," said Smashie. "We really are."

"Mmm-hmmm," said Willette. "You better think of a way to make it up to Mr. Bloom."

"We will," said Dontel. But the look on his face was determined, not meek. Whatever he had figured out about the jar was giving him confidence.

The children filed back into Room 11. Ms. Early looked at them. "Why do you all look so unhappy?" she said.

"We're not," said Siggie. "Some of us are mad."

"Oh. Well. Let's see if we can put aside those feelings for now. It's time for writing. We can talk at the end of the day if you all feel like we need to."

"No. It's fine," said Jacinda. "Smashie thinks it's fine, too, don't you, Smashie?"

"I think it's very fine," said Smashie hastily. She couldn't bear for Ms. Early to know that she had been rude to Mr. Bloom. *What if they talked in the staff lounge?* she worried. *What if Ms. Early winds up not liking me anymore, either?* If only they could solve this case! Then the kids would forgive them and she and Dontel could have a real heart-to-heart with Mr. Bloom.

Ms. Early furrowed her brow briefly. But all she said was "Fine. Get out your notebooks and use this time to generate thoughts, or if you're working on a story, keep going. I'll come around to check in with you as you work."

"Come on, Smash." Dontel grabbed Smashie's wrist and their notebooks and tugged her into the reading corner.

"Tell me everything!" Smashie demanded. She couldn't imagine working on her writing before she knew what Dontel had remembered.

"Smashie," said Dontel, his voice deep with

mystery, "I don't think the thief is stealing the jars to sabotage our musicale. I think we have stumbled onto *enormous intrigue!*"

"Intrigue!" breathed Smashie. "I love intrigue! But how do you know it's intrigue?"

"The jars!" said Dontel. "Remember when Charlene passed around the first one? The one that rolled away and that Mr. Bloom found?"

"Yes," said Smashie. "Dontel, are you thinking that the second jar rolled all the way from our room to the gym and behind the basketball bin wheel? Because I think that goes along with my idea about Charlene's mother somehow making them jet-propelled!"

"Smashie," said Dontel wearily, "the jars are not jet-propelled. Believe me, I'd be glad if they were. But no. This is something else. There's something different about this jar. This is definitely the second jar, the one Charlene used to make Joyce's first hairdo — that hair heart."

"How do you know?" asked Smashie.

"Because" — Dontel paused — "I remember that the first jar, the one Mr. Bloom found that Charlene used to make your music note, only had the words about Herr Goop on it. But the second jar had *numbers* on it. And so did the third jar—the one Joyce's mom bought. I remember because I looked at them all."

"I noticed that, too," said Smashie. "Why does that matter? And how do you know this was the second jar and not the third?"

"Because I remember that one of the numbers on that second jar was 77!" said Dontel. "I didn't remember the other numbers, but I remembered that one."

"Dontel," said Smashie, "I mean this in a nice way, but—who cares?"

"Hear me out, Smashie," cried Dontel. "Because even though I don't remember the numbers on the third jar—the one that Joyce's mom bought—I know that there was no 77. Why would the numbers be different?"

"OK," said Smashie. "If only we had the rest of the numbers on that jar you found in the gym, we might be able to figure it out!"

"We do," said Dontel smugly. "I wrote down all the numbers that were on that jar. I have them right here, in my Investigation Notebook."

"Dontel," said Smashie, "you are a wonderful investigator."

"Only sometimes," said Dontel modestly. And he opened his notebook to the page where he had written down the numbers.

26 99 77

The two investigators stared at the numbers. Then slowly, they turned to look at one another. Smashie knew their minds were as one.

She was right.

"Smashie," said Dontel, "I think this is a secret code! And that means —"

"There is not just one thief! *Two* people must be involved!"

CHAPTER 21

Another Breakthrough

"Yes! One perp is communicating with another via a code!"

"A different message on each jar!"

"Why, though? And how can we crack their code?" Dontel wondered aloud.

"Smashie and Dontel," called Ms. Early, "are you two working on your writing?"

Smashie and Dontel jumped. "We were just brainstorming, Ms. Early!" said Smashie. But she squirmed. Were she and Dontel telling too many lies? Or at least half-truths? Honesty was important to Smashie. But she knew that if she told Ms. Early what they were doing, her teacher would take away their Investigation Notebooks and tell them to stop being silly and to work on their school tasks. But still. Smashie's shoulders hunched.

The door to Room 11 opened. But for once it wasn't Mrs. Armstrong come to shout at them. It was Miss Dismont. She crossed over to Ms. Early.

"Our Hair Extravaganza and Musicale will suffer if we don't have the children in those perfect hairstyles," she said quietly. "Should we spring for those ingredients ourselves?"

"They cost so much," Ms. Early said. "I don't know that we can buy enough for what we need. Or raise enough in a quick bake sale, to be honest with you."

The two women sighed. Smashie and Dontel exchanged glances.

"We better work on our writing quickly and get to investigating right after," Smashie whispered to Dontel as the door shut behind Miss Dismont. "I have to fix the spelling in my story, anyway. I have a bunch of hard words in there." Smashie's story was a long one, full of shoes who wished they lived on other people's feet. "Can I borrow your tiny dictionary? I can't remember exactly what that word is for when things act like people."

"Sure," said Dontel, and fished the fat little book out of his pocket. "It's all yours."

Smashie took the dictionary. Then it fell from her fingers.

"Is it *anthropomorphic*?" asked Dontel.

But Smashie wasn't listening. "Dontel," she breathed, "I know the secret of the code!"

CHAPTER 22

Code Cracking

"Dontel," she whispered. "*Dontel! I've got it!*"

"Tell me!" said Dontel desperately. But Ms. Early was already turning their way with a warning look. The two friends had to get to work on their writing.

"Oh, why can't it be bus time?" wailed Smashie, very quietly.

It was a miserable wait until the final bell signaled the end of the day. But at last it came, and the two friends hurried down the aisle of their bus to find a seat in the very back.

"You behave back there," Mr. Potter warned.

"We will!" cried Smashie. "We're only going to be working."

"Well, I hope you're going to work on some kind of apology to Mr. Bloom," sniffed Willette as they went past her. "Maybe you could think about making him some cupcakes or something."

"Good idea, Willette," said Dontel.

But Smashie was too excited to think about apology baking, even for Mr. Bloom.

"Spill it, Smash!" said Dontel as soon as they were seated. Mr. Potter put the bus in gear and they were off.

"It was your dictionary that gave me the idea," said Smashie. "Dontel, how many letters are in the alphabet?"

"Are you kidding me?" asked Dontel.

"Never mind. I know you know there are twenty-six. But what I mean is, look what happens when I number the letters!"

In a fresh page of her notebook, Smashie wrote them out.

1.A   2.B   3.C   4.D   5.E   6.F   7.G
8.H   9.I   10.J   11.K   12.L   13.M   14.N
15.O   16.P   17.Q   18.R   19.S   20.T
21.U   22.V   23.W   24.X   25.Y   26.Z

"What if each number stands for a letter?" Smashie cried. "Maybe the numbers spell out something amazing!"

"Like what?" asked Dontel.

"Maybe secrets to a treasure!" said Smashie, her eyes glowing. "Treasure with enough in it to buy ingredients for Mrs. Stott to make us more goop! Or maybe it's a plea for help from some kind of magical being! And we will have to storm some kind of lair to save him or her! We'll need swords and shields! And armor!"

"Smashie," said Dontel.

"Oh, fine," said Smashie. She knew he was about to tell her that her imagination was running away with her.

"I like the thinking," said Dontel. "And the first number in the code is 26. That works; it's a Z. But the next one is 99. There aren't 99 letters in the alphabet!"

But Smashie shook her head. "No, Dontel! Not the whole number. I think we need to take each digit *individually*! A 2, then a 6. Then 9, then 9. Then the 7, and the 7."

"Ah!" Dontel's eyes flashed. "I like it! Let's get to work."

There was a pause as their pencils flashed bumpily across the page, on account of the bus bouncing about.

"Well," said Dontel, looking at his work, "there goes that theory."

"*Theory* is a good Investigator Language word,"

said Smashie. "We should add that to the list. But you are right about it not working."

For, using Smashie's method, the would-be code spelled out

BF II GG

"It makes no sense," said Dontel. "But that was a good idea, Smash."

Smashie was staring at the page.

"Maybe it stands for something," Dontel suggested. "Maybe they're acronyms. You know, like how NASA, our national space program, stands for National Aeronautics and Space Administration."

But Smashie shook her head.

"Wait," she said. "WAIT!" And she rewrote the numbers, but this time, instead of putting them side by side, as they had been on the jar, she wrote them in a vertical list.

26
99
77

"Now let's write it out!" she cried. And before Dontel could even catch up with her, Smashie had already written it in her notebook.

    B F
    I I
    G G

"Isn't that the same thing?" asked Dontel, puzzled. "No!" cried Smashie. "Read it up and down!"

    B   F
    I   I
    G   G

Dontel's eyes widened. "Ohhh!" he said. "BIG FIG! Smashie, you were right!"

"So were you," said Smashie. "And I think I know what it means!"

CHAPTER 23

Fig Work

"The TrueYum Grocery Mart," said Smashie firmly.

"What? Why the TrueYum? I never noticed they sold super big figs before."

"I don't know if they do, either," said Smashie. "But, Dontel! Think of the sign just by the entrance!"

Dontel's mouth dropped open. "It is a *picture of an enormous fig!*" He looked at Smashie in admiration. "Smashie," he said, "I thought you were losing it with the magical-being stuff, but this is excellent. You are something else!"

And they slapped each other's hands with their hands.

"But how will we get there?" Smashie wondered aloud. "It's way outside the parameters of where we're allowed to go alone."

"My grandma," said Dontel firmly. "She told me this morning that she needs to go shopping this afternoon. We can just . . . encourage her to take us."

"We can offer to help," said Smashie. "Then we won't feel guilty about not telling the whole truth." But she did feel a bit guilty.

"I think we are doing it for the greater good, don't you?" said Dontel. "Something is happening, and it's up to us to catch the perp!"

"That's true," said Smashie, comforted somewhat. "Oh, well. Let me get permission to come over to your house."

"You can't play at Dontel's today," said Grammy when Smashie got home. "Mrs. Marquise and I have to go shopping. We're cooking for both families tonight and we need supplies."

Smashie could scarcely believe her luck. She bounced up and down in front of Grammy.

"That's great!" she said. "I really want to go!"

Grammy looked at her strangely.

"You hate grocery shopping," she said. "You always say it's like being trapped in the boringest place in the universe, and you complain and thrash about until we can leave."

"Not today," said Smashie. "Me and Dontel want to make brownies. May we? For tonight's dessert? We can get the ingredients."

"Brownies?" said Grammy doubtfully. "Do you have to make a mess in the kitchen today, of all days? We're having the families eat together so we can help you and Dontel get ready to lead your first rehearsal tomorrow."

"We want to take some brownies to Mr. Bloom as well."

"The custodian? Why? Did you make a big mess at school?" Grammy was stern.

"No," said Smashie. "At least, not the kind of mess you mean."

"Hmm." Grammy looked at her thoughtfully. "All right. As long as it's okay with Lorraine." That was Dontel's grandma. The cooking for the night's supper was to happen in the Marquise kitchen.

"Thank you!" cried Smashie, hugging Grammy around the waist. She ran to the front door and flung it open.

"She said yes!" she screamed across the street at Dontel in his yard.

"My grandma did, too!" screamed Dontel back. And they air-high-fived across the street. The two grandmothers, standing in their respective doorways, exchanged looks and sighed. They very much saw eye to eye when it came to Dontel and Smashie.

"All right," said Mrs. Marquise as they pulled into the parking lot of the TrueYum. "You two find us a cart with four good wheels while Sue and I go look at the produce."

"We'll investigate things about produce, too!" cried Smashie, looking at Dontel meaningly.

Dontel elbowed her quiet as the two women made

their way into the store. "Quit almost giving us away! Who needs produce for brownies, for Pete's sake?"

"Sorry, Dontel," said Smashie. "I was just enjoying the coincidence." And the two children sidled casually over to the rows of carts, which stood handily below the TrueYum fig sign.

"Well," said Smashie, "that certainly is a big fig. But I don't see anything suspicious about it, do you?"

"No," said Dontel. "I guess I don't really get what we are supposed to do now. Let's test some carts and think." For the TrueYum carts were old, and the grandmothers were very picky about having carts with four working wheels.

Creak, crark, went Smashie, testing a cart.

Crark, creak, went Dontel, testing another. "This is no good." He stopped, hand on the cart handle, and this time, it was his jaw that dropped.

"You have an idea!" squealed Smashie.

"Shh!" whispered Dontel fiercely. "There are passersby! And who knows who might be involved?"

"You are right," said Smashie. She lowered her voice to a whisper. "What are you thinking?"

"Look at the top of the sign."

Smashie looked at the sign, which lay flush against the wall of the market. "I don't see anything," she confessed. "Except hinges."

"*Exactly,*" Dontel whispered. "And that means . . ." He snaked his fingers under the bottom edge of the sign. "You keep watch."

Smashie looked around the parking lot. No one was looking in their direction.

Dontel lifted the edge of the sign. The hinges creaked. He drew in his breath sharply.

"What?" cried Smashie, and came around to look.

But there was nothing there. Nothing, except a piece of tape to which a scrap of paper was still stuck, clearly torn off from a larger sheet that had been fastened there.

"We're too late," said Smashie. "Somebody already got what was taped there!"

"We *are* too late," Dontel agreed. "But we were right, Smashie! These thefts were never about the goop!"

Smashie nodded. "The jars are clues to something much bigger! It was about secret messages the whole time!"

"Yes," said Dontel. "But what are the secret messages? What do they say?"

"And why use our goop to send clues? Maybe we have another enemy who really does want to wreck our musicale as well as be involved in intrigue!"

But before Smashie could start up her imagination on the topic, the doors to the TrueYum flew open. "Are you two ever coming in with that cart?" Grammy demanded. "Or do you want Mrs. Marquise to walk around with her arms full of tomatoes for the next half hour while you chitchat?"

The shopping over, Smashie and Dontel were in the Marquises' kitchen, working on the brownies.

Smashie slapped her forehead. "I completely forgot to ask you. Why didn't you let me take the jar from under the basketball bin? Why did you want to leave it there?"

"Because," said Dontel, cracking the first egg into the bowl, "it was placed there so carefully I knew it was meant for someone. It was no accident."

"But who could it have been meant for?"

"The code receiver," said Dontel.

"I know that," said Smashie. "But who could that be?"

"I have no idea," Dontel admitted. "But we can watch to see if another one appears there under the indoor basketball bins again. Maybe we'll even catch who comes to collect it in the act!"

"We would have to have a hot pursuit!" Smashie's mind filled with the image of her and Dontel racing after the suspect, arms pumping, legs churning, and finally grabbing the collar of the perp and turning him or her over to the authorities. Or at least to Ms. Early. And then maybe she would be so proud of Smashie that she would let her sing in the musicale! Smashie's Investigator Suit looking so much like an Officer of the Law Suit would be good for catching a perp like that. Though, she supposed, now that the kids were onto that particular suit, she couldn't wear it again.

"Who do you think left the jar there?" said Smashie. "Charlene's mom? She's the one who makes the goop and puts it in the jars and labels them. It makes sense that she's the one putting the codes on them."

"But why would she?" said Dontel, cracking another egg.

"I don't know why," Smashie admitted. "But if it was her, we might not have noticed because she did it in a black sneaky Thief Suit!"

"You always think people are doing things in black sneaky Thief Suits."

"Fine. Maybe she wore camouflage, then," said Smashie, and she began to stir the batter with all her might. "She could have elbowed her way across the room on her stomach and we'd never see her! She could reach up, steal the jars, and—"

"Smashie." Dontel picked up the rubber scraper. "I am going to have to stop you. This makes no sense. If she wanted those particular jars, she would have just kept them at her house. My goodness. And besides, she and Charlene were both really happy we were going to use her goop so more people would come to her hair salon."

"Ugh," said Smashie. She knew Dontel was right. "Fine. But then I am going back to my magical-being theory." And she held the bowl while Dontel sighed and scraped the batter into the pan.

• • •

Dinner between the two families eaten, the adults and kids assembled in the Marquises' living room. Dontel's mother started the music. Smashie and Dontel began to practice teaching everybody how to dance the Pony.

"Fling your arms like this!" Smashie shouted to the adults while Dontel counted out the beat.

"Do your feet like this!" Dontel shouted while Smashie critiqued the grown-ups' form.

And everybody flailed their arms and Ponied until it was time for Smashie, her mother, and Grammy to go home.

"I hope the kids aren't too mad at us to let us teach them," said Smashie under her breath as everybody said their good-byes at the door.

"They won't be. We have those apology brownies. I think Mr. Bloom and the kids will forgive us."

"I sure hope so. Otherwise, we have some dark days ahead."

CHAPTER 24

Rehearsal

It was after lunch the next day and Room 11 was beside itself about their first day of rehearsal for the musicale. Ms. Early and Miss Dismont led the two classes in a giant line down the hall to the auditorium. The third grade knew it was supposed to be quiet as it filed through the halls, but it was very difficult to do today. Whispers erupted everywhere.

"I've been working so hard on my song!" said Tatiana.

"Me and Lilia from Room 12 have, also," said

Alonso. "We've been practicing after school every day since the day we signed up to sing."

"Dontel and I have been practicing teaching the dances, too," said Smashie, who was wearing her Choreographer Suit (multicolored sequins up the sides of her jeans and spelling out DANCE-A-GO-GO! across her shirt).

Willette sniffed. "I don't know how people are going to learn to dance from people who are mean to people," she said.

"Willette! We apologized!"

"We baked apology brownies for Mr. Bloom!" Dontel cried. "But he's absent today because he's at a UFO conference, so we can't give them to him."

"But we will," said Smashie. "As soon as he's back!"

"Oh," said Willette. "Well, that is really nice of you. Sorry, Smash. I promise I'll work hard to learn the dances."

"Speak for yourself," muttered a boy from Room 12. "I don't know that brownies are enough to make up for a man's hurt feelings."

"Or not having any goop to make cool hair with," said another member of Room 12.

Smashie and Dontel exchanged bleak looks. If that boy was still mad at them about accusing Mr. Bloom, who knew how many other children still were? And of course the entire third grade was still worried about the missing Herr Goop, too. Even the teachers were. Put those worries together with everybody being mad at them about taxing Mr. Bloom — well, it was hard enough to perform sixties go-go dances in a living room with only Dr. Marquise and Grammy. Imagine what it was going to be like with a lot of upset third-graders!

"We better solve this mystery of the jar codes — quick!" said Dontel. "We have to redeem ourselves."

"I agree," said Smashie earnestly. "If we do that *and* give Mr. Bloom the apology brownies, I think people will like us again."

"I like you," said Alonso unexpectedly behind them.

"Thanks, Alonso," said Smashie.

"We like you, too," said Dontel. But he and Smashie exchanged warning looks. They had better be more careful about being overheard.

The class filed into the auditorium and sat in a large circle on the stage.

"We know you all have been working on your acts at home," said Miss Dismont. "And that's great. Our musicale is coming up so quickly we don't have nearly as much time to rehearse as we'd like. So we're excited to see how your numbers are coming along!"

"Dontel, have you chosen a dance to go with your speech yet?" asked Ms. Early.

"Yes," said Dontel. "We're going to do the Shimmy. It's not as good as . . . that dance we aren't allowed to say, but people do wiggle around in it, and that is still a lot like the way some scientists think parts of the universe are moving."

"Splendid," said Ms. Early. "So here is how our rehearsal will work. I will stay here and practice with the first few singers and their backup people. That keeps Dontel available, so Miss Dismont will bring the rest of you to the gym so he and Smashie can begin to teach you the dances for our inter-act inter-ludes. How does that sound?"

"Good," said some of the children.

Others were silent.

"They brought Mr. Bloom brownies," Smashie

heard Willette whisper to Jacinda. "I think they really are sorry."

"Hmm," said Jacinda. "We'll see."

"We also want to mention," said Ms. Early, "that we have a lot of parents and family members who have volunteered to help us as well. Charlene, would you like someone to help you do the hair? Assuming, of course, that we find our missing goop?"

That's a lot to assume, thought Smashie. *No matter how hard Dontel and I are trying to investigate.*

"I think I'm okay alone," said Charlene.

"Regardless," said Ms. Early, "there are a lot of heads in the third grade. I think we need some support for you, doing all that hair."

"I can help," said Carlos shyly.

Charlene blushed and said nothing.

"Wooo-OOOO!" went several children.

"Stop it!" said Charlene. "You're embarrassing me."

"That is very nice of you, Carlos," said Miss Dismont. "I'm sure Charlene is grateful."

"She's not acting it," said Smashie to Dontel.

"That's the way it is with like-liking someone sometimes," said John, who had overheard. "You act mad to cover up that you like-like the person you like-like."

"Again with the like-like," sighed Smashie.

"My mom can help me, Ms. Early," said Charlene. "She's taught me everything I know about hair sculpting, anyway, and I know she'd be glad to help us."

"If we get the goop back," said John.

"Yes," said Charlene. "If we ever do." Her face was strained.

"Splendid," said Ms. Early. "And we can always have Carlos on hand for backup."

Carlos tried to hide his smile. But he couldn't.

"All right, dancers! Line up behind Smashie and Dontel, and let's get to that gym," said Miss Dismont.

Smashie and Dontel stood up. Smashie couldn't help casting a longing eye at the singers. Wouldn't it be *useful* to have someone who could sing as loudly as Smashie could, doing one of the songs?

But Ms. Early only said, "See you later, Smashie." It was clear that she was not thinking of the advantages of having a loud singer in the musicale. Only the ones who were already signed up.

Smashie sighed.

. . .

It wasn't easy for Smashie and Dontel not to run to the basketball bin and check to see if the jar of Herr Goop was still there. But they couldn't, not with all the kids around. *It will have to wait until we can find an opportunity,* thought Smashie.

Cyrus pushed his glasses up on his nose. "Just how hard are these dances, you guys?" he asked nervously.

"They are wicked easy," Smashie promised.

"As easy as being rude to Mr. Bloom?" asked Charlene.

Smashie was taken aback.

"Charlene! They apologized!" Willette was becoming something of their champion in the matter.

"Thank you, Willette," said Dontel.

"Children," said Miss Dismont, "these arguments have to stop. We have work to do, and there's no reason why it shouldn't be fun, despite our worries! Walter, man the music player. When I say hit it, go for it! And Smashie and Dontel can start us off! All right—HIT IT!"

Walter hit it.

"Left, right, left!" Smashie shouted, showing the feet for the Pony. She was glad for last night's practice at the Marquise house. "Right, left, right!"

"Now swing your arms!" shouted Dontel, demonstrating.

Clunk.

It was Cyrus. The children gathered around him as he lay on the gym floor.

"I can't do the arms and legs at the same time," he said miserably.

"Sure you can," said Dontel, helping him up. "This is only your first time. Come on. I'll help you." And he drew Cyrus off to the side to give him some private instruction.

Wait a minute, thought Smashie. *I know how I can get a glance at those basketball bins!*

As Miss Dismont organized the remaining kids into a line, Smashie crossed the room and stood near the basketball bins. Dontel glanced at her, eyebrows raised.

"Pony toward me!" Smashie shouted at the other kids. "And hit it!" The children Ponied toward her beautifully, with Miss Dismont, a game if clumsy dancer, bringing up the rear.

"I'm getting it, Smashie!" yelled Willette.

"You're doing great!" yelled Jacinda. Smashie's shoulders relaxed. Maybe the dance was winning Jacinda over. Maybe it was only Mr. Bloom she had to worry about now. Oh, why did he have to be absent? Still, she had her opportunity to look at that jar and could not be distracted now.

Dontel clearly understood what Smashie was up to. "Now Pony back toward me!" he called from the other side of the room, with a nod at Smashie, and the children dutifully pivoted and Ponied back whence they had come.

Smashie seized her chance. With everyone else's back to her, she squatted down, and sure enough, there, behind the wheel of the basketball bin, was a jar of Herr Goop. But it was not the second missing jar that they had seen before. For this one contained several three-digit numbers, not just the two-digit numbers like the last jar. The numbers on the jar read:

212 75 125 256

Could this be the third missing jar? The one Dontel had said had different numbers on it?

Smashie's fingers itched to take it. But she knew she couldn't, not without being noticed. And her time was short.

Quick! Take a mind picture, Smashie told herself. And she did. Staring at the numbers, she repeated them under her breath until she could see them as clearly in her mind as they were written on the jar. Then, before the children could finish dancing and turn back to her for instructions, Smashie Ponied back to the group herself and prepared to teach the children the next dance.

CHAPTER 25

Smashie and Dontel Think Things Through

When the rehearsal was over, the dance children rejoined the ones who had been practicing musical numbers, and they all walked excitedly back into their rooms.

"WOW!" said Tatiana. "Alonso, you and Lilia sounded great!"

Alonso looked down modestly. "Thanks," he said. "It's a real good song."

"Dontel," whispered Smashie under the cover of

the babble around them, *"there was a jar under that basketball bin!"*

"I knew it!" whispered Dontel back. "Was it still that second one that was stolen?"

"No!" whispered Smashie. "I think it was the *third!*"

But before she could continue, they had reached Room 11, and Ms. Early was talking to John. "I wish we had time to hear your piece, John," she said.

"You will," John said miserably. "Next rehearsal. I promised my dad."

"All right, Room 11," said Ms. Early as they entered and settled. "Time for math."

"Oh, Ms. Early!" cried Charlene. "I have good news! My mom just left us a jar of replacement goop in the main office!"

"Yay!"

"What?"

"That's great!"

"Can you regoop me?" asked Joyce. "I had to wash out the roller-skate wheels, and now my hair is like a group of potatoes again."

Room 11 was very hopeful.

But Dontel and Smashie were puzzled.

"Huh?" said Dontel. "I thought your mom didn't have any more ingredients."

"She said she got the ingredients from a mysterious benefactor," said Charlene. "Someone sent her money with a note saying they heard about our troubles and wanted to help us out with our musicale Herr Goop."

"Well, that was very nice of the . . . of the . . ." Cyrus started.

"Mysterious benefactor," Charlene helped him.

"Yeah," said Cyrus. "That."

Ooh, thought Smashie. *A mysterious benefactor!* She imagined a Rolls-Royce pulling up to Charlene's house and a tiny monkey with a fez presenting Mrs. Stott with a check.

"But we still won't have enough," said a worried Tatiana. "That's just one jar. We need three!"

"And I still think someone took the others!" said Siggie.

"Hmm," said Ms. Early. "Well, that was very kind of . . . of someone to help your mother, Charlene. But do try to be sparing. We can't expect more gifts like this. I wish we knew who it was, so we could send a thank-you note."

Smashie squirmed in her chair. This was great news, but when was Smashie going to get to tell Dontel about the code she'd seen?

"Do my hair next?" begged Billy. "Lemme see the jar!"

"Sure." Charlene passed the jar to John, who passed it to Dontel, who passed it to Billy, who made the very unwise decision of flinging it back to Charlene, only to hit Patches's cage instead.

"Billy Kamarski!" said Ms. Early. "That is not acceptable!"

Willette sprinted pell-mell to the back of the room, yelling, "PATCHES! ARE YOU HURT? DON'T WORRY! I AM COMING!"

"Willette, is Patches all right?" asked Joyce.

"Yes," said Willette, leaning over Patches's cage. "He seems fine. He is eating his pellets very nicely."

"How about the goop?"

"The jar didn't break," Willette said.

"Phew!" went much of Room 11.

"You're telling me," said Willette.

"Splendid," said Ms. Early. "Room 11, I don't know if it is because of our musicale or what, but you're not acting entirely like yourselves. And I am not sure I like it."

"I really am sorry," said Billy. "I just got excited about my hair."

"I know. But throwing things is not acceptable." Ms. Early sighed. "Let's all calm down and get ready for math."

But a rumbly undercurrent of Room 11 continued as the children found their spots to work, and the relief of some about the replacement goop mixed with the muttering of those still concerned about the missing jars and impending musicale.

Smashie and Dontel headed to the reading corner once again with their papers and their Investigation Notebooks. Smashie had rid herself of her satin jacket after the censure of her classmates, but her tool belt was still in place. After all, she reasoned, it was mostly pencils, pens, and markers in there, besides her Investigation Notebook. If you really thought about it, how could she do without it? She needed most of those things most every day in school.

And not having the jacket part of her suit on did make the other kids think she had given up on the investigation after the Mr. Bloom fiasco, so that was good, too. If the code maker or receiver were in Room 11, they'd never know Smashie and Dontel were still hot on their trail.

"Who do you suppose the mysterious benefactor is?" Smashie wondered aloud as they walked. "Because I think it is a wealthy gentleman with a trained monkey. I think—"

"Smashie," said Dontel, saying her name in the way he used to quell her when her imagination threatened to take over. "It's more likely to be a friend of Mrs. Stott's, one of Charlene's relatives, or an adult here at school who knows about our situation. . . . Who knows? But let's hurry with our math. Because both of us have things to report!"

"Eep!" said Smashie, and she put aside ideas about trained monkeys as the two friends worked their math problems quickly and efficiently.

"I need to tell you what I noticed just now, when we were passing the new jar of Herr Goop from kid to kid," said Dontel when they were done at last.

"What? Tell me!"

"The label was made out of a little thicker paper, maybe, but *there were no numbers on it!*" Dontel leaned toward her. "You know what that means?"

"No," said Smashie honestly.

"It means the perp isn't leaving any old jar of goop we get under those basketball bins. Just ones with the code!"

"That must be true!" said Smashie. "Because the jar I found under the basketball bin today did have numbers! Only"—she leaned closer—"*not* the same ones as on the second jar. That's why I think it must be the third jar—the one Joyce brought in!"

"I *knew* it," said Dontel. "The ones we are finding by the basketball bins are the only ones that matter!"

"So the perp must be somebody who has access to our basketball bins," said Smashie. "Let's put that on the Opportunity List."

And they added it carefully.

THINGS THAT MUST BE TRUE ABOUT THE
PERSON, LIKE OPPORTUNITY
1. They had to be in the musicale planning
meeting circle because that's when the first jar
of goop went missing.
2. They had to be in math when we did the
tens and ones review because that is when the
second jar of goop went missing.
3. They have access to the bins where the
basketballs are kept.

"Wait a minute," said Smashie. "That is a terrible clue. Everybody in the entire school has access to those bins."

"True enough," said Dontel. "But it makes that list longer, and we both like that. Let's get to the code numbers! Did you write them down?"

"I couldn't do that without all the kids noticing," said Smashie. "So I memorized the numbers. We can write them down now."

And turning to their CODE-FIGURING-OUT PAGE, Smashie wrote:

212 75 125 256

Dontel copied the numbers carefully.

"Are you sure you remembered it right?" he said doubtfully.

"Of course!" said Smashie. "I danced it into my brain after I memorized it. And if that isn't motion sparking a notion, I don't know what is."

"Well, something is not working," said Dontel. "Look what happens when you start figuring it out."

"I'm doing it horizontally first," said Smashie. And, using her list of the numbered alphabet letters, she wrote:

BAB GE ABE BEF

Then she rearranged them vertically, as they had for the BIG FIG.

B A B
G E
A B E
B E F

"Ugh!" Smashie fell back against the pillows in the reading corner and flung her arms in the air. "My code doesn't work anymore!"

Ms. Early interrupted her class. "Some of you seem to be having a little trouble," she said. "Let's talk together as a group and review what we've been going over in math. How can we make 638 using only tens and ones?"

"Use 63 tens plus 8 ones!" offered John.

Under the cover of their classmates' speech, Dontel and Smashie carried on. "I'm afraid you're right," whispered Dontel. "The code doesn't work."

"Not unless BGAB is a word," whispered Smashie back. And she sat up again, only so she could fall dramatically back to the cushions once more. "And BGAB is not a word!"

"Nope," said Dontel. "Neither are AEBE or BEF. It must be a new code altogether."

"Or a new language!" cried Smashie. "Maybe it is the language of a magical being we have to save after all! We will have to translate. But first we have to learn the language. Dontel, you should—"

"Smashie and Dontel!" Ms. Early was standing

before them. "I am very disappointed in the way you are not focusing on your math. Separate, please. Immediately!"

Anguished, Smashie and Dontel exchanged looks. But there was no arguing with Ms. Early. Miserably, Smashie went back to their table while Dontel stayed where he was in the reading corner.

The investigation would have to wait.

CHAPTER 26

Bus Codes

Across the room, Cyrus shouted. "Done!" he said. "Is it okay if Charlene practices on my hair, Ms. Early? I was very thorough with my math work."

"I don't see why not," said Ms. Early. "As long as Charlene has done a good job on her math as well?"

"I sure have!" said Charlene, showing Ms. Early her work. And so it was that after a few minutes, Charlene had lengthened and molded Cyrus's hair into a pony head, complete with flaring nostrils, to match the Pony dance.

"Wow!"

"Looks amazing!"

"Just like a real pony!" said the students in Room 11, craning their necks.

"It does," said Ms. Early. "Wonderful job, Charlene. Now, everyone get back to your math. It's almost time to pack up for the buses."

Smashie's mouth fell open. She had an idea. One that might break the code wide open. Her idea had not been inspired by Charlene's beautiful work. No.

It was inspired by math.

Smashie reached the bus before Dontel and saved him a seat. They didn't even say hello before they took out their Investigation Notebooks.

"Dontel," Smashie whisper-shouted, "I think I have cracked the code!"

"Spill it, Smash! What's the new code?"

"That's just it!" cried Smashie. "It *isn't* a new code!"

"What?" said Dontel incredulously. "Smashie, I thought we already determined that AEBE was not a word."

Smashie shook her head. "Get out your math work," she demanded.

"We're done with that! I want to do this!"

"Believe me," said Smashie. "They go together." And they both took out the math sheets they had worked on in class.

"Our problem is that we were looking at the *digits* of each number," said Smashie. "But we should have been looking at *how we can build the numbers in different ways.*"

"What do you mean?"

"Well, look at the first code," said Smashie, "26 99 77. We took each digit separately, but what we should have done was think about what they mean in the number! It's how many tens and ones can fit in the number, not just the digits!"

Dontel furrowed his brow. "But doesn't that amount to the same thing?" he asked. "You still wind up with BIG FIG."

"For that one, you do," said Smashie. She took out her pencil. "But not for the third Joyce jar!"

"Sure you do," said Dontel. "If you go by the number of hundreds, tens, and ones, because there are three-digit numbers in there."

"No," said Smashie. "That's just what I mean! We still need to look at the numbers just in terms of how many *tens* and *ones* we can use to make it! NOT using the hundreds! Look at the numbers of the code."

212 75 125 256

"Now think about what we've been doing in math! How many tens can fit in 212?"

"Ohhhh!" breathed Dontel. "I get it! You could see it as 2 hundreds and 1 ten and 2 ones —"

"Or you could see it as *21 tens and 2 ones!*"

"Smashie! You've got it!"

"I know! Once I remembered how every hundred

is 10 tens, I realized all the hundreds numbers could be thought of as being made up of tens, too! Just like Ms. Early has been helping us learn!"

"So the code is really . . ." Dontel scribbled furiously.

21, 2   7, 5   12, 5   25, 6

"Yes!" said Smashie. "And now we can match it up to the alphabet numbers." And they did. Horizontally, it spelled

UB GE LE YF

But vertically, it was

U B
G E
L E
Y F

"UGLY BEEF!" they cried in unison. They slapped each other's hands with their hands.

"But what the heck is ugly beef?" said Smashie.

"I don't know," said Dontel. "But I'm sure we can figure it out. What could it be? A bad-looking hamburger?"

"Or a misshapen pot roast?"

"And where do we even find gross-looking meat?"

Smashie thought. "Do you think we should go back to the TrueYum and look in the meat department?" she asked. "I don't think I can get my mom to go shopping again when Grammy just did the shopping yesterday."

Dontel stared at her. And then he laughed. He laughed so hard Smashie grew quite annoyed.

"I didn't know the idea of my grammy shopping was so funny," she said.

Dontel stopped. "No," he said, wiping his eyes. "I just figured out the UGLY BEEF!"

"What?"

Dontel finally stopped laughing, but his voice was still tinged with merriment. "Smashie," he said, "the BIG FIG referred to a sign, right?"

"Yep," said Smashie. "The TrueYum."

"Well, this one does, too, I think." And he dissolved in giggles again.

"Where the heck is there a sign of a bad-looking steak in our town?" Smashie demanded.

"You have to stretch the meaning of UGLY BEEF just a little," said Dontel. "Like, where does beef come from?"

"Cows," said Smashie. *"Oh! Cows!"*

"Exactly!" cried Dontel. "The Dairy Delight! That terrible-looking cow on the sign!"

"Oh, but I don't think that's quite fair of the code maker," said Smashie. "That poor cow looks more weird than ugly."

"I think *weird* would have been harder to work into the code," Dontel pointed out. "The way they do the code, both words have to have the same number of letters."

"Well, I feel bad for that cow," said Smashie. "The poor thing can't help how she was painted."

"Sad or not," said Dontel firmly, "we have to get over there as soon as we can. Maybe this time we can get there before the code receiver does! We can crack the mystery wide open!" His shoulders sagged. "But how can we get to the Dairy Delight? All these places are too far for us to go to alone!"

"I have an idea," said Smashie. "Get permission to come over to my house and come as soon as you can."

CHAPTER 27

Tasty Clues

"Mom!" Smashie was delighted to see her mother. Usually Mrs. McPerter was still at work when Smashie got home, and Smashie and Grammy held down the fort until she came around five. But Friday was her half day.

"How was school, Smashie?" asked Smashie's mom. "How are things with the Hair Extravaganza and Musicale? I can't wait to see it. I am so proud of your dancing."

Smashie said nothing. Somehow, her mother's

warm words about her dancing stirred up Smashie's disappointment at not being chosen to sing once again.

"I know," said her mom. "You're still sad that you aren't singing in the musicale."

"It's just that . . . I always have to do the dances in shows. I never get to sing."

"That's so," said her mother.

"And I'm a good, loud singer, too," said Smashie. "I really know how to make myself heard in the back of the room!"

"That you do," said Smashie's mother. "It's a disappointment, I know. But the best thing for you to do *now* is to do your very best with the job you were given. And in the meantime, you can practice your singing so that you are ready for the next opportunity that comes along to sing at a school function."

"Hmm." Her mother had a point. There was no use pining if she couldn't sing this time. But if she practiced enough, maybe there would be another chance someday, and Smashie would be ready for it.

"Mom," she said, "have you ever heard of the song 'Endless Amour'?"

"I have," said Mrs. McPerter. "But I'd love to hear your version." Smashie beamed and began to sing.

The teacups on the dining room shelf quivered.

Dontel arrived at last, somewhat out of breath from running from his house. "Sorry I wasn't here earlier, Smashie. Hello, Mrs. McPerter. How are you?"

"Just fine!" Smashie's mother beamed. "So good to see you!"

"You just missed me singing," said Smashie.

"Oh," said Dontel.

"Mom?" Smashie asked. "For a special treat, what do you think about all of us going to the Dairy Delight for ice cream?"

"I can think of nothing better to celebrate my half day," said Mrs. McPerter. "Dontel, I'll call your grandma at once."

Not long after, permission secured from Dontel's grandmother, Dontel and Smashie found themselves with Smashie's mother in front of the Dairy Delight ice-cream shop. And sure enough, there was the sign for the shop swinging on a hook next to the door. The sign was filled with the snarling face of a cow, which was attached to a cow body that was so out of proportion it looked like a pork chop. All in all, she did not look very much like a cow who was happy that her milk was to be made into a sweet treat.

"Well, Smash?" asked Smashie's mom. "Are you coming in or do you want to do Surprise Me cones?"

"Surprise Me cones!" Smashie cried. Surprise Me cones were when Mrs. McPerter went in alone and came out with cones of the most exciting flavors on offer. And once you chose a cone, it was yours with no backing out. Sometimes the results were lovely, like the time Smashie got chocolate-cookie swirl with rainbow candies. And sometimes the results were awful — like the time she wound up with raisin-fizz sherbet with filbert sprinkles. But the possibility of the cone being wonderful made the ice-cream getting much more exciting than just choosing a regular old flavor herself.

Dontel thought so, too.

"And it gives us time to get a good look at that sign," he said as Smashie's mother disappeared into the ice-cream shop.

They turned their attention to the sign. This sign was free-swinging, so it was easier to see the back. But, just as had happened at the TrueYum, they were too late. Once again, there was only a piece of tape and a corner of paper stuck to the back of the sign to show that a message had ever been placed there.

"Darn!" said Smashie. "Too late again!"

"Or are we!" cried Dontel, and pointed down the street. A child-size figure in black was darting away from the Dairy Delight as fast as its legs could carry it, a piece of paper waving in its hand.

"And you always make fun of me for thinking that people steal in black sneaky Thief Suits!" cried Smashie.

But Dontel was not paying attention. "Smashie," he said, "I think I know who that was!"

CHAPTER 28

Ice-Cream Deductions

"Butter brickle with mint crumbles, chocolate brownie with macadamia smash, and rainbow sherbet with butterscotch topping!" Mrs. McPerter stood before them triumphantly with the cones. "Who wants what?"

Smashie gnashed her teeth. Her mother's timing was terrible. Who could eat ice cream at a time like this?

Dontel, was who.

"Count me in for the rainbow sherbet!" he cried, and ate his zestily while Smashie fixed him with a glare during each stony lick of her own choice, the butter brickle. But even distracted by the investigation, she had to admit it was delicious.

"Thanks, Mom," she said.

"No problem," said Mrs. McPerter. "I'm glad I got the chocolate one."

I'd rather have gotten the perp, thought Smashie. *But I guess that will have to wait, too.*

On the way home, Smashie's mom had her Bon Jovi music playing and was singing along with it at the top of her lungs.

"Now I see where you get that from," said Dontel, next to Smashie in the backseat. "The loudness."

"Yep," said Smashie. She lowered her voice. "But we can at least talk about the case while she's singing. Dontel, who do you think it was running away with the paper?"

Dontel chomped his final bite of cone and wiped his mouth with a napkin. "Carlos," he said finally.

"CARLOS!"

Mrs. McPerter's singing broke off. "Are you asking me to play Carlos Santana instead, Smash?" she asked.

"Um, yes?" Smashie hazarded. She had better control her shouting if they were going to get any good investigating done on the way home.

The music switched and Mrs. McPerter started singing again to the beautiful riffs of Santana's guitar.

"How do you know it's Carlos from Room 12?" whispered Smashie.

"His build," said Dontel firmly. "And he's such a good runner. And whoever it was, was really covering ground!"

"Yes," Smashie agreed. "We should have given chase!"

"No way," said Dontel. "He had way too good of a head start. Besides, your mom would have been worried sick if she had come out and we weren't there."

"That's true," said Smashie. "But what I don't get is, why Carlos? What's in those notes?"

"I don't know," said Dontel. "But I do get who's leaving the codes!"

CHAPTER 29

The Perp!

"What?" cried Smashie. "*Who?*"

"Think about it logically. Who else is learning about tens and ones with three-digit numbers? Who else has access to the jars? Who else might have been there when Joyce came in for her haircut, and who always has tabs on the goop jars at school?"

Smashie smacked her own self on the forehead. "Of course! Charlene!"

"That's exactly who I think," Dontel said.

"Now that you say it, I know you're right!" said

Smashie. "You know why? That was a *kid's* hand-writing of the numbers—not a grown-up's! And I've been Charlene's partner millions of times in math, and those numbers I saw today were in her handwriting!"

"Good thinking, Smashie. I think Charlene is taking the jars herself and planting them where Carlos can find them, decode them, and then go get her messages!"

Smashie paused. "But why doesn't she just give him the jars?" she asked reasonably.

"He's in Room 12," Dontel reminded her. "We never really see them. She couldn't count on that."

"Wait," said Smashie. "There's a big flaw in this. Charlene was super mad when the kids said she like-liked Carlos. So why would she be leaving him notes if she doesn't like-like him?"

"Well, remember what John said about how when people like-like someone sometimes they pretend like they don't?"

"Not really," said Smashie honestly. "I never pay much attention when people talk about like-liking each other."

"Me, either," said Dontel. "But that stuck with me."

"But it still doesn't make complete sense," said Smashie. "Because why would Carlos wear a black sneaky Thief Suit to get the notes?"

"Maybe he is embarrassed to get the notes and wants to be in disguise," said Dontel. "You know, the way you like suits. Maybe the black sneaky Thief Suit helps him."

But Smashie was not thinking about suits. "I will be disgusted if all our hard work turns out to be just about like-like notes," she said.

"Ugh," Dontel agreed.

"Bluck," said Smashie.

"Well," said Dontel, "we have to make sure we are correct in our thinking. We don't want to get carried away in the wrong direction."

"But I kind of like to get carried away," said Smashie as Mrs. McPerter continued to wail along with her music.

"I know," said Dontel. "But I want to be sure. I want to check our facts."

"There is only one sure way to do that," said Smashie.

Dontel's eyes widened. "Tax Charlene?" he said incredulously.

"No," said Smashie. "Well, I mean, maybe we can tax her a little bit. I am kind of scared about taxing since the Mr. Bloom fiasco." Which reminded her that she still had the apology brownies going stale in her cubby at school. Ugh. "But what I mean is that"—she gulped—"I think I am going to have to get a haircut."

CHAPTER 30

Smashie Makes a Sacrifice for the Case

"Smashie." Dontel looked at her hard. "Are you sure? Your hair is already pretty—" He stopped.

"What?" asked Smashie.

"Nothing," said Dontel hastily. "I think it's really noble of you. You are sacrificing your head for the investigation."

"Well, someone has to. There may be important clues in that salon at Charlene's house!"

Dontel looked at her with deep respect.

Smashie cleared her throat. "Mom?" she asked loudly over the guitar riffs coming from the front seat. "May I please go get a haircut?"

"Right now?" asked her mother, startled.

"I just think I really need one. I feel a little shaggy."

"But you always—" Dontel started.

Smashie glared at him. "Plus, Charlene Stott's mom is trying to start up her own salon, so it would be good to bring her business."

"Okay, I guess," said Mrs. McPerter. "I can call Charlene's mom." She pulled the car over and got out her cell phone. "Hello? Mrs. Stott? Oh, Charlene! How are you, honey?"

Dontel and Smashie exchanged significant looks.

"This is Smashie's mom, and she'd like to come for a haircut. Now? Great! I'll bring her right over." She disconnected her earbud as Smashie's heart began to pound. "Okay, kid. Off we go. Charlene was very happy you were coming to her mother's business. Dontel, I'll drop you home first."

"Smashie," said Dontel fervently, *"thank you."*

Smashie nodded.

Do I have time to make a Like-Like Note Detecting Suit?

she wondered wildly. But she knew she didn't. She would have to imagine herself in one instead. And, closing her eyes, she pictured herself with Joyce's hair heart and her mother's other satin jacket. That one was red. But she also gave herself a badge that said INVESTIGATOR on it. If she couldn't wear one in real life without giving herself and Dontel away, in a mind suit, she certainly could. It gave her quite a boost of confidence.

"I won't see you over the weekend," said Dontel. "We are going to visit my other grandma. But don't worry. I'll be thinking about the case the whole time. And your head."

"Smashie McPerter! I haven't seen you in ages!" Mrs. Stott was wearing a cheerful pink smock decorated with different kinds of hairdos. Updo, beehive, side swept, ponytail — the four hairstyles danced in rows across the smock.

"It's nice to see you, too, Mrs. Stott," said Smashie. Her heart was pounding. How terrible would she look after this haircut? Would the other members of Room 11 make rude remarks about her hair the way

they had the other day when it was especially sticky-outy? Or would they forgive her the rest of the way about Mr. Bloom because she had made this sacrifice to save the musicale?

"I'm set up in the basement," said Mrs. Stott. "Come on down. And let me get a smock on you, too."

Smashie's smock turned out to be black with cupcakes of different flavors marching across. *Perfect,* thought Smashie. *Sneaky black like the Thief Suit, and delicious because of cupcakes.*

"Sit down in the chair and lean back, Smashie," Mrs. Stott instructed her. And she upended Smashie in the chair and began to wash her hair.

"Yow!"

"Too cold?"

"Too hot!"

"Sorry about that!" Mrs. Stott adjusted the water.

"Is Charlene home?" Smashie asked as Mrs. Stott tipped the chair back up and readied her scissors. *Be brave,* she said to herself. *Remember, it's only hair and hair grows back.*

"Nope," said Mrs. Stott. "She went to the park with

her little sister and aunt and cousins. But maybe she'll be back by the time we're done."

Smashie was a little ashamed to find herself relieved that she wasn't going to have to tax Charlene. Especially all by herself. And in front of Charlene's own mother, no less.

All around the room were pictures of people with beautiful hair sculptures.

"Did you style all of those, Mrs. Stott?" asked Smashie.

"I sure did!"

Snip, snip, snip.

Smashie's eyes widened in alarm. Quite a lot of hair was falling on the floor.

"You love it already, don't you?" Mrs. Stott was smiling proudly.

"I . . . I really like those sculptures," said Smashie lamely. It was too hard to tell a white lie in this instance. What was going on with her bangs? And what was happening at the back of her head? How did Joyce bear this, and why would anyone even want to?

Because I am trying to be an ace investigator is why,

Smashie told herself firmly. But her reflection in the mirror was worried.

"I can't tell you how thrilled I am that you kids like our Herr Goop so much," said Mrs. Stott, snipping away.

"We love it," said Smashie.

"Well, we had just enough ingredients left that I made you kids another jar last night. It's not quite full, but it ought to be enough to get most of the kids' heads done. Charlene bagged it up to take in to school on Monday." Mrs. Stott nodded at a little bag on the countertop.

Smashie couldn't help wiggling in her chair. A jar of goop prepared by Charlene! It was sure to have the next code on it. But could she get ahold of it without Mrs. Stott noticing? If she could, she and Dontel would be able to intercept the message before Carlos! *Although, intercepting some like-like note wouldn't be all that fun,* Smashie thought. Still, though. They had to be sure that was all it was.

"Did you make that jar from ingredients left over from the ones you bought with the money from your mysterious benefactor?" she asked, hoping Mrs. Stott would talk about what it was like to receive a check on a salver from a trained monkey.

"My mysterious benefactor?" Mrs. Stott laughed. "I wish. No, this is from the very last of what I had left anyway. Last I'll ever make, I guess, at least for a while." She sighed. "I have to admit, Charlene and I are pretty proud of that goop."

"You should be," said Smashie. "Those hair sculptures in the pictures are beautiful. And Charlene is great at using it to turn our hair into shapes, too."

"I agree," said Mrs. Stott. "She has a real gift." She sighed. "I hope this business picks up enough that she can style hair here if she wants to when she's older. It's hard work striking out on your own, believe me."

"Yes," said Smashie, who, even though her brain was churning to figure out how to get her hands on the Herr Goop on the counter, was feeling very much alone in that haircutting chair, watching brown hanks of hair fall all around her.

"But it was the right thing to do," said Mrs. Stott. "I had to leave Mr. Garcia's salon."

"Mr. Garcia?"

"You know. Carlos's dad. Oh, right, I forgot. He's in

the other third-grade class. Nice kid. But his dad—"
Mrs. Stott shook her head. "He was not happy at
all about my hair goop. I overheard him say that he
believed *he* had the rights to it because I must have
made it in his salon with his ingredients! 'There's no
way she made this in her own kitchen,' I heard him tell
one of the other stylists. 'That woman doesn't know
thing one about what ingredients work well together.'
Well, let me tell you something—I do make our goop
in my own kitchen with my own ingredients, and I
do, too, know what ingredients work well together on
human hair!" Mrs. Stott was getting quite worked up.

But so was Smashie. "You mean, you left that salon
because Carlos's dad was unfair to you?"

"Yes, I did."

Smashie was unused to a grown-up talking to her
about things like this. But her mind was whirling.
"Would you say that you and Charlene are . . . mad
at Mr. Garcia?"

"We sure are," said Mrs. Stott. "But I'll show him!
I've got haircutting skills, too, not just sculpting! I'll
make a success for myself and market our goop on
my own! You mark my words!"

"I am," said Smashie. "I am marking them."

What the heck was going on? If Charlene was as mad at Carlos's dad as her mother was, there was no way she was sending Carlos like-like notes. Charlene loved her mom and was really trying to help her start this business. But then why *was* she sending Carlos notes? Nothing made any sense anymore. Smashie needed to talk to Dontel.

"Hey," said Mrs. Stott unexpectedly. "Why don't you take this jar of Herr Goop with you and bring it to school on Monday? It'll save Charlene a trip down here to the basement."

"All right," said Smashie dimly, scarcely believing her luck as Mrs. Stott dropped the little bag of Herr Goop in Smashie's lap.

Mrs. Stott finished blow-drying Smashie's hair and stepped back. "What do you think?"

Smashie's jaw dropped.

Never mind Charlene and her reaction to finding out that Smashie had the goop. How was Smashie going to face Room 11 with her hair looking like this?

CHAPTER 31

School Bus Brainwork

"Red satin?" asked Dontel on the bus on Monday morning. The two friends were very happy to see each other after a weekend apart. "Smashie, have you changed up your Investigator Suit jacket?"

"Yes," said Smashie firmly. "The kids might be on to me in that blue one, but this one will throw them off!"

Dontel hesitated. "Will it, though?"

"It will. I am not doing the tool belt part. I think that would give it away, if I wore both together again."

"Hmm." Dontel looked at Smashie's head. "Are you going to take that hat off?" he asked. Smashie was wearing her winter knit cap. It was awfully hot, but the alternative was worse.

"Never. Dontel," she said, "the sacrifice might have been Almost Too Much."

Dontel shook his head sorrowfully. "I really appreciate what you did, Smashie. I thought of you all weekend. You are a . . . a *noble* investigator."

"Maybe noble for no good reason, though," said Smashie. "Dontel, I think we were wrong about most everything!" And she told him all about what Mrs. Stott had said about why she left Carlos's dad's salon. "She and Charlene do not like the Garcias at all! So dollars to doughnuts, this is not a matter of like-like notes at all. I have no idea what's going on! Are you positive it was Carlos who was running away in the black sneaky Thief Suit?"

"Yes," said Dontel firmly. "It was his exact build, and you know what a good runner he is."

"Well, could we be wrong about the Charlene part? Is there anyone else who fits all those things you said about having access to the jars and knowing who is coming?"

"I can't think of a soul," said Dontel. "At least, not a kid soul, and we know it's a kid." As he did every day, he took his sandwich out of his lunch bag and began to eat it. "Plus, Mrs. Stott would have to be a little nutty to leave notes for a kid all over town."

"Yes," said Smashie. "And I'm sure we're right about Charlene for another reason, too." She paused significantly. Dontel stopped chewing. "Mrs. Stott told me she had just enough ingredients left to make us a close-to-full jar. Which was on the counter. Bagged by Charlene. And guess who Mrs. Stott gave it to, to bring to school!"

"You?" Dontel said incredulously.

Smashie nodded.

"Well, there it is, then!" said Dontel. "High five, even if we don't get what the heck is going on!" They slapped each other's hands with their hands. "Smashie," said Dontel, swallowing a bite of sandwich, "there *is* a code on the jar, isn't there?"

"There sure is!" said Smashie, and with the air of a

magician pulling a bunny from a hat, she pulled the jar out of its little bag for Dontel to see. "I checked! But don't worry. I resisted temptation and saved it to work on together."

"Thanks, Smash," said Dontel.

"Sure thing. You'd do the same for me."

"I would," said Dontel.

Then, carefully, just in case other third-graders on the bus were looking, Smashie turned the jar around so the label was visible. And sure enough, there was a code, written in Charlene's hand.

16 211 203 155

"Let's get to work!" And the two friends busied themselves on the code page of their notebooks.

"That makes it 1 ten and 6 ones," said Dontel. "Then 21 tens and 1 one."

"Then 20 tens and 3 ones," Smashie finished. "And 15 tens and 5 ones!"

"You know, I just realized that you can just look at the first two numbers of the three-digit numbers, and then the last one, and solve the code the same way," Dontel pointed out.

Smashie gave him a level look.

"I like it the math way better," she said. "More complicated."

"More thinky," Dontel agreed.

Smashie turned to her own notebook.

1, 6   21, 1   20, 3   15, 5

"And that makes . . ." Smashie translated busily with the help of her numbered alphabet page.

AF UA TC OE

"Which makes . . ." Dontel wrote it vertically.

A F
U A
T C
O E

"AUTO FACE!" they said together. But Smashie remembered to whisper this time. This was no time for her to shout again and tip their hand.

But the two friends paused. "What the heck is an auto face?" Dontel wondered out loud.

"Maybe that front part?" Smashie suggested. "The way the headlights can look like eyeballs sometimes?"

"But that's every car . . ." Dontel objected. "Maybe it's a car someone decorated," he offered. "You know, like people sometimes put antlers and a red nose on the grille at Christmas."

"Or those fake eyelashes," Smashie agreed. "But, Dontel, if it's an actual car, it's hopeless! We'd have to walk all over town looking at every car until we found one with a face on it, and you know our grandmothers will never let us do that!"

"True." Dontel sighed. "That would take us way outside the parameters of where we are allowed to go alone." Then he sat up straight. "Smashie. Charlene—if it's her, and we are sure it is—has only hidden her papers on shop signs so far."

"You are right," Smashie agreed. "That is another clue!" But before they could write that down on their

CLUE page, Smashie sat bolt upright. "Dontel! *I know what sign it is!*"

"Lower your voice!" said Dontel, and Smashie subsided. But there was no stopping the excitement in her voice, even as she dropped it to a whisper.

"Cyrus's parents' mechanic shop!" she said. "Grammy brings her car there whenever she can't fix it herself." Grammy was very good at fixing things. Or, generally she was. Sometimes her fix-its had to be fixed. "And the Hulls' shop has a sign with a cartoon car on it! *With a face!*"

"You're right!" Dontel slapped Smashie's hand with his hand again. "That's it! I love that sign. But how will we get there? We have to get to it before Carlos does."

"Yes," said Smashie. "But, Dontel, we are in luck! Because you know where Hulls' Auto Body is?"

Dontel's face broke into a beam. "At the end of our block!"

"Within our parameters!" For the two friends were allowed by their grandmothers to bike to the end of their long block and back. Any farther than that and special permission was required but was rarely forthcoming.

"Yay!" said Smashie. "And we live much closer to that auto shop than Carlos does. There's no way we won't beat him this time!"

"Yes!" said Dontel. "And when we see whatever is on that message, maybe we'll get some kind of clue about Charlene's motive for leaving him these notes."

"I really do hope that this is not just like-like notes," said Smashie. "And that Charlene isn't just sneaking around to send them to Carlos because her mom is so mad at Carlos's family, and this is all a silly waste of our time after all."

Dontel nodded slowly. "It could well be. It's just . . . I feel like it must be something more. Why else would Carlos dress up in—"

"A black sneaky Thief Suit?" finished Smashie. "I don't know. Maybe Carlos knows her mom and his dad would feel betrayed if he and Charlene were friends, so he's hiding it, too." She sighed. "I guess we ought to tax them both."

"No," said Dontel unexpectedly. "Because if it is Charlene, and it's something more interesting—"

"Or more full of intrigue—"

Dontel nodded. "—than just stupid like-like

notes, we don't want to throw her off. We can't let her know we're onto her. We need her to plant that auto face note—"

"Or we'll never know!"

Dontel squirmed in his seat. "This day better go fast!"

The bus arrived at school. "Everybody out!" said Mr. Potter, and with a hiss, the bus doors opened and the children piled out.

"They're going to make me take off this hat, aren't they?" said Smashie sadly as they went into the school yard.

"I'm afraid so, Smash," said Dontel sympathetically, swallowing the last of his sandwich. "Don't worry. I'll be there to stick up for you."

CHAPTER 32

Undercover Ocean Waves

"Do any of you need help figuring out what to wear for your numbers in the musicale?" Ms. Early asked her class at the start of morning meeting. "Only two days until our performance!"

"You know I'm wearing real roller skates for my song, right?" asked Tatiana.

"I certainly do," said Ms. Early, making a check mark on her clipboard. "Smashie and Dontel, do you need people to wear—" She broke off. "Smashie. Hat."

Smashie wilted.

"Do I have to?"

"You do."

Smashie tugged off her hat.

"Thank you," said Ms. Early. "As I was saying, do you and Dontel need the kids to wear anything in particular for the dances?"

Smashie's jaw hung open. Ms. Early must be being tactful. But as she looked around the class, no one looked shocked. Or mean. Or any of the ways she had worried about this morning coming to school with Stott-cut hair.

She turned to Dontel.

He raised his eyebrows and shrugged. "It doesn't look that different."

"What?" Smashie squawked. "You guys," she addressed Room 11, "don't you see how my hair is? I got one of Mrs. Stott's haircuts! I look nuts!"

"Hey!" said Charlene.

"No more nuts than that time you cut your own bangs when we were in preschool," said Dontel.

Smashie felt betrayed.

"Dontel!"

"Calm down, everyone," said Ms. Early. "Smashie, I am sorry we didn't notice your hairdo." She hesitated. "But under the circumstances, I think that is a positive thing."

"It looks great!" said Charlene. "See, you guys? I told you my mom can cut hair!"

"Well, Smashie's hair is always pretty messy," said Siggie.

"*Hey!*" Now Smashie's feelings were the ones that were hurt. "I comb it every day! I just have sticky-outy hair!"

"Siggie Higgins," said Ms. Early, "we do not make personal comments about others."

"Siggie does," Smashie muttered.

"Smashie," said Ms. Early.

"Sorry," said Smashie.

"Smashie, my mom said she gave you a jar of goop to bring to school. Do you have it?" asked Charlene.

"Yes, I do," said Smashie. And she passed the little bag over to Charlene.

"Yay!" cried Room 11.

"That brings us back up to two jars!"

"Will that be enough, Charlene?" asked Ms. Early.

"I'll have to use it very sparingly. And it might not last. But we might just squeak by."

"Ms. Early, can Charlene help Smashie style her hair now?" asked Dontel. "I know we don't want to waste any goop, but Smashie has . . . a complicated head of hair. And after all, we are talking about what we are wearing for the musicale."

"All right." Ms. Early gave her permission. Dontel and Smashie exchanged looks.

"Great!" said Charlene, and the two girls went to the back of the classroom. Smashie's heart pounded. Alone with one of the perps!

"I'll make it look super, Smashie. Remember, it lengthens as well as molds," Charlene promised. "Even if I have to use it sparingly."

Tchah! thought Smashie. *We could be crawling with plenty of goop if you were honest and quit giving the jars to Carlos!*

But "Thanks" was all she said. She watched carefully to see if Charlene looked at the code, but Charlene barely glanced at the jar before she swiveled off its lid and scooped up a bit of the lovely lavender-and-lilac-scented goop and went to work.

"Check you out!" said Charlene, giving her one of the symmetry mirrors.

Looking in the mirror, Smashie saw that this time her hair had been turned into rippling ocean waves, perfect for the Swim dance.

Charlene beamed. "You love it, don't you? Our goop is the best!"

Smashie couldn't help but beam back. She did look terrific. And Charlene was so happy. Could anyone be that happy when they were involved in code-based intrigue?

But she only said, "Thank you, Charlene! Your styling is as good as the goop. I'll just stick the jar here in my backpack so we have it ready when we need it."

She looked hard at Charlene. But Charlene only said, "Great," and went to the sink next to Patches's cage to wash the goop off her hands.

Sure enough, though, by the time lunch rolled around, the jar was gone.

"We're onto something," Smashie said to Dontel. "But I'm not going to make a big fuss about the jar being missing. I don't want anyone else investigating or for our class to be even more on edge."

"It's terrible when our class is on edge," agreed Dontel. "Fine. We'll proceed as if nothing has happened."

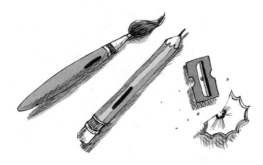

CHAPTER 33

A Wild Suspect!

The class filed to art for the last period of the day. Mr. Flange stood before the art supplies, his mustache hanging down in glorious ringlets over his mouth.

"Mr. Bloom did lend him his goop after all!" whispered Dontel.

"Did he ever," said Smashie. "Hello, Mr. Flange. You . . . look very nice today."

Mr. Flange gave a nod. Between his mustache and Smashie's hair, the air was filled with the scent of lavender and lilac.

Mr. Flange gestured silently toward the paints and the rolls of mural paper.

"You want us to make the signs and banners for the musicale?" Joyce said.

Mr. Flange nodded.

"Then we better get going."

The children put on the big shirts they used to protect their clothes and got to work.

Dontel and Smashie went to cut several lengths of mural paper. They planned to paint on them the names of each of the sixties go-go dances the class was to perform, and tape the signs up on the wall of the stage behind the dancers.

"Scissors, please," said Smashie.

"Smash," said Dontel firmly, "we don't have time for you to go to the nurse today. You are going to have to let me do the cutting."

Smashie opened her mouth to squawk, but then shut it. Dontel had a point.

"Oh, fine," she said.

Dontel went to work.

"Let's make the letters in the Pony sign look like ponies!" said Smashie.

"Great idea!" said Dontel. "We can use the horse on the front of your Investigation Notebook as inspiration."

Smashie fished it out. She lowered her voice. "And we can update our Suspect List again," she said. "Should we put Mr. Bloom on and then cross him out? Just as a record of our mistake?"

"I don't think so," said Dontel. "We really didn't suspect him. And then it all turned so awful."

As if on cue, Joyce appeared over their shoulders. Her hair was in two braids. Now that her roller-skate wheels had been washed out, she only had her regular hair until the night of the musicale. The braids did a lot to hide the terrible haircut.

"Did you give Mr. Bloom the apology brownies yet?" Joyce demanded.

"No!" said Smashie. "He's still at his conference!"

"Oh," said Joyce. "Well, don't forget to do it when he comes back. The kids are only forgiving you because you said about the brownies."

"Jeepers," said Dontel. "It's a lot harder to get forgiven in our class lately."

Joyce sighed. "We've been through a lot," she said.

"I mean, the whole Patches thing . . ." She shook her head. "I'll remind the kids how you helped with that." Her face grew a bit hard. "Even if the taxing part didn't go so well."

"Thanks, Joyce," said Dontel. "We better get back to work on our signs."

"Me, too," said Joyce. "I'm doing John's 'Come On Over to My Place' sign, and I don't even know what to do for it. Do I do all the food the person in the song lyrics offers? Or do I do a lot of dwellings?" She wandered back into the main section of the art room, still muttering.

Smashie tapped her horse notebook. "I'll sketch," she said. "You add Charlene to the Suspect List."

Dontel did.

SUSPECT LIST
1. ~~John~~
2. ~~Billy~~
3. Charlene

"Her motive probably *is* boring old like-like," said Smashie. "But she is shorter-tempered than usual these days, too. Is that what people are like when they write like-like notes?"

"Well, remember that she's pretty worried about her mom's business getting off the ground, too," Dontel pointed out. He looked thoughtful. "We'll know more when we see what she has taped to the car sign. Let's look at the Opportunity List and make sure that Charlene fits all those, just to be thorough." And they flipped to that page in their respective notebooks.

THINGS THAT MUST BE TRUE ABOUT THE
PERSON, LIKE OPPORTUNITY
1. They had to be in the musicale planning
meeting circle because that's when the first jar
of goop went missing.
2. They had to be in math when we did the
tens and ones review because that is when the
second jar of goop went missing.
3. They have access to the bins where the
basketballs are kept.
4. Smells like the goop. (The thief probably
smells like the goop because that is a super
strong smell that sticks with you.)

5. *Is working on third-grade math about the number of tens in a three-digit number.*
6. *Has access to the hair goop jars.*

"Yep, yep, yep, yep, yep, and yep," said Dontel, thwapping the page. "Charlene fits them all. Plus, she has plenty of motive."

"She does," agreed Smashie. Then she looked up sharply. "Dontel!" Her voice was distressed.

"Smash? What's wrong?"

Smashie looked at him, horrified. "Was at the planning meeting? Access to the basketball bin? *Learning about the tens and ones?* WAS IN CHARLENE'S HOUSE? *SMELLS LIKE THE GOOP? AND HAS A MOTIVE, TOO?*" She aimed her styled head at Dontel. Her eyes were anguished. "Dontel, we can't shy away from facts! Someone else fits those criteria!"

"Who?" said Dontel.

And underneath Charlene on the Suspect List, Smashie carefully wrote:

4. *Me*

CHAPTER 34

Dancing Detection

"Smashie," said Dontel, "you are getting carried away. Again!"

"I am not!" Smashie made as if to tear at her hair. She encountered goop and stopped, mindful of not messing up her ocean-wave hairdo even in this terrible moment. "Don't go easy on questioning me! I could be a hardened criminal!"

Dontel pinched the bridge of his nose and shook his head. "Smashie, you suspected yourself in the Patches investigation, too."

"I know! But this time is worse! I fit all those criteria *and the motive, too!* I've been very angry that I haven't been allowed to sing a song! We thought that was Billy's motive, but—"

"*Smashie.*" Dontel's voice was very firm. "I will ask you straight out. Did you make up that code and put them on the jars and then leave some kind of notes all over town?"

Smashie looked at her lap.

"No," she said. "I guess I didn't do that."

"Exactly," said Dontel. "I didn't think we had to put all that on the list of things that are true about the perp, but I suppose with you we—"

"Dontel," said Smashie, "I am sorry. You know how I get carried away."

"Yes," said Dontel patiently. "I do. Now, let's just get this day hurried up and done with so we can get over to Hulls' Auto Body and get that note before Carlos does!"

Signs painted, materials cleaned, bus ride taken, and permission to ride bikes secured, Smashie and Dontel were now riding pell-mell down the street to

Hulls' Auto Body. It didn't take long at all before they saw the familiar sign hanging from the side of the building, its cheerful blue cartoon automobile with goggly eyes beaming at potential customers.

"I'm glad it's on the side of the building," said Smashie, slowing her bike. "We'd be awful visible around it on the front with no adults with us as an excuse."

"True," said Dontel. "Come on! We have to hustle to get to that message before Carlos comes to get it, whatever it is."

And they leaped from their bikes and sidled over to the sign.

"Hey, you two!" It was Cyrus. Smashie jumped a mile. "What the heck brings you guys here?"

Smashie's mind went blank. She looked helplessly at Dontel.

"Smashie here was remembering about how you were confused about that one step in the T-t-t-emptation Walk," Dontel stuttered. "And so we biked over, hoping you might be here so she . . . so she could help you."

"Really?" Cyrus was pleased. "I'd like that! Let's go

around back and practice. I'll feel dumb doing it out here in the open."

"Sure thing," said Smashie, and she and Dontel exchanged meaningful looks. Dontel nodded, and Smashie headed around the back of the building to help Cyrus.

"It's scoop, scoop with your arms, then turn and scoop, scoop. Scoop, scoop," directed Smashie, trying to see over Cyrus's scooping arms to the side of the building where Dontel was, she hoped, busy with the sign.

"Like this?" Cyrus scooped and turned.

"Two scoops," said Smashie. "That's it!"

"Scoop, scoop, turn, scoop, scoop, turn! Smashie, I think I have it!"

"I do, too," said Smashie warmly. She was pleased with his progress, but what was Dontel up to? Did he get the message? Was he having a clash of wills with Carlos even as she spoke?

The answer came quickly. "Smashie." Dontel was breathless from his run from the side of the building. "We, uh, better get home before our grandmothers think we went past our parameters."

"That's too bad," said Cyrus. "I'd really like some more help with these dances."

"Come over after supper," Smashie invited him. "I can help you then. Tomorrow's dress rehearsal, after all, and we want you to feel confident!"

"Yes," said Dontel, his voice full of meaning. "Like I feel right now. Very confident."

Smashie looked at him, her heart pounding. Dontel nodded quickly, once.

"Great," said Cyrus. "I'll ask my mom. See you later!"

"See you later!" And the two investigators hopped on their bikes and began to race home.

They were just in time. For behind them, a black-clad child appeared in the distance, making its stealthy way toward the sign with the cheerful blue automobile with the goggly eyes.

"Do you have it?" Smashie asked breathlessly. "I thought I'd never be done helping Cyrus with that dance!"

"Nope," said Dontel.

"*Nope?*" cried Smashie. "Dontel! It wasn't there?"

"It was there, all right." Dontel puffed as he rode. "But I couldn't take the paper. Otherwise Charlene and Carlos would know someone was onto them. But I'll tell you what," he said as they turned into the Marquise driveway. "I copied down the message into my Investigation Notebook. *And it is no like-like note.*"

Smashie squeaked. "What is it?"

Dontel looked at her hard. "Intrigue," he said. "We are up to our necks in intrigue."

CHAPTER 35

Science Clues

Smashie could scarcely wait for Dontel to pour them each a glass of milk and make a plate of cheese and crackers before he showed her what he had found.

"You two settling in for homework?" called Dontel's grandmother from the sitting room.

"We are working hard!" Dontel called back. "And we better," he said more quietly to Smashie. "This message is weird. It looks even more codey than the jars."

And he flipped open the page in his notebook, and there was his copy of the message he had found taped to the back side of the sign. "Right behind the goggly eyes," he said.

To YOU:
500 MG OLIVE OIL
100 MG EXTRACT OF LAV

Be prepared to receive final note during the 194 169 213 45 194.
Be careful! No one must know about this!
Signed, ME

"What the heck?" said Smashie. "I know what olive oil is. But what's lav? Isn't that short for, like, *lavatory*? The bathroom? Maybe this is where she makes it! Maybe the bathroom is her secret lab, and *Charlene* is a rocket scientist working on making the jars turbo-charged! Maybe—"

"No!" cried Dontel. "Smashie, don't you see? It's short for *lavender!*"

"Oh!" Smashie said. "You mean it's—"

"Yes!" cried Dontel. "It's the recipe for the hair goop!"

"But Dontel, I know there are way more ingredients in the hair goop," said Smashie. "Mrs. Stott talked about having a ton of ingredients in her kitchen. Two is not a ton."

"But Smashie," said Dontel, "this is the third note! Maybe the recipe is being broken up into pieces!"

Smashie drew in her breath. "Dontel!" she said. "This *is* a like-like note!"

"What do you mean?" said Dontel.

"Well, I don't know what all those kooky letters and shapes with the lines mean," said Smashie. "But I do know that if Charlene is giving the recipe for her mother's goop to Carlos—"

"Whoa," said Dontel. "You mean you think she like-likes him so much that she is betraying her own mother?"

"Yes," said Smashie firmly. "I think she is passing along the recipe for the goop because Carlos's dad thinks he has the right to be the one making and selling it since she invented it when she worked for him!"

"That is pretty low-down," said Dontel. "Do you really think Charlene is doing that?"

"Every bit of the evidence points that way so far!" cried Smashie. "She has opportunity and motive and all those things we talked about. And from what you all say, when people like-like people, they do weird stuff."

"But this is terrible," said Dontel.

"Only the Charlene part," said Smashie. "The rest is great!"

"What do you mean?"

"I mean, we can decode the place where it says Carlos will receive the 'final note' and intercept it! And protect Charlene's mom!"

"And hope it brings Charlene to her senses," said Dontel. "I mean, if you like-like someone, can't you just write them a note to that effect?"

"Maybe that's what the hexagons mean."

"Well, look at that!" Smashie and Dontel jumped.

It was Dontel's grandma, come into the kitchen, her thumb holding her place in her John le Carré spy novel. "Are you two doing chemistry in the third grade?"

She was peering at the note.

"Chemistry?" asked Smashie. "What is that?"

"It's a branch of science that tells us what things are made of. And how those things are connected. You see a lot of those lines and hexagons when you represent the chemical structure of something."

Dontel looked at Smashie. Smashie looked at Dontel.

Mrs. Marquise smiled and shook her head. "That's probably too old for you two," she said. "But someday you'll study all that, if you stick with your plan to be an astrophysicist, Dontel."

And she left with a glass of milk and plate of crackers of her own.

"Science," breathed Smashie.

"*Yes!*" said Dontel. "I'm more convinced than ever that this is part of the formula for the hair goop! It's being systematically stolen, and it's up to us to stop it!"

"Let's get to work on that code," said Smashie grimly. And they turned to the CODE-FIGURING-OUT PAGE in their notebooks and wrote:

194   169   213   45   194
19, 4   16, 9   21, 3   4, 5   19, 4

"I'll do the tens; you do the ones," said Dontel. And before they could shake a stick, they had it:

"SPUDS," said Dontel.

"DICED," said Smashie.

"Spuds diced? SPUDS DICED?" Smashie cried. "What the heck does that even mean?"

"Let me look in my little dictionary," said Dontel, fishing it out of his pocket. He flipped to the letter *S*. "'*Spud*,'" he read. "'Another word for potato.'"

Smashie slapped her forehead. "I should have known that!" she said. "My grammy calls them that sometimes. But 'diced'? What could that mean?"

"When my dad cooks and the recipe says diced," said Dontel, "it means he cuts the stuff up into little cubes."

The two were silent, thinking of potatoes in little cubes.

"What the heck?" said Smashie. "How are we going to find a pile of potatoes in little cubes?"

"Maybe it's another sign?" Dontel suggested. "Like, breakfast hash browns or something on a sign for a restaurant?"

But neither of them could think of a single sign like that nearby.

"Dontel," said Smashie, "the note says that Carlos will receive the final note *during* the SPUDS DICED. How can you receive something *during* a sign, for heaven's sake?"

"I surely do not know," said Dontel. "Smashie, have we come this far only to fail?" He looked at her in despair.

Smashie looked back at him. Then she sat up straight. "Let's dance it out. Motion sparks the notion, says Ms. Early, and it's worked for us before!"

"Let's do it!" They Ponied. They Swam. They Temptation Walked, Skated, and Shimmied. And then Smashie stopped short, forcing Dontel to bump into her as he Shimmied. "Sorry," he said. "I got distracted and was thinking about my astronomy piece that I'm speaking in the musicale."

"It doesn't matter!" Smashie cried.

"Well, it does to me," said Dontel, stung.

But Smashie shook her head and began to laugh. "I don't mean your piece, Dontel. I meant it didn't matter that you bumped into me because I know what SPUDS DICED means! It's the last dance! It's *the Mashed Potato!*"

CHAPTER 36

A Plan

"Motion does spark the notion!" cried Dontel. "Smashie!"

"Exactly! Charlene's plan is to give Carlos the last part of the formula during the Mashed Potato. During our very own class musicale!"

"Why couldn't she just say that plainly?" Dontel asked. "SPUDS DICED is a heck of a way to get the idea across."

"Well, she is limited by the tens and ones code," Smashie pointed out. "She can use any letters for the first word, but the second word has to be made up of only the letters *A* through *I*, because you can only have up to nine ones in a number in the ones spot."

"That's true. Good math thinking, Smash. In that case, it's pretty clever," said Dontel. "But still sneaky! We have to stop her! Mrs. Stott is too nice to not be the one to make and sell their goop!"

"Do you think Carlos's dad put Carlos up to it? Is he the nefarious type?" Smashie wondered.

"I don't know him," said Dontel. "I go to a barber."

"Well, we can figure all that out at the musicale. But for now, we better plot! How are we going to intercept that last note?"

"Motion sparks the notion," said Dontel again firmly. "We are going to have to tweak the choreography of the Mashed Potato so you and I can make sure that Charlene can't get to Carlos."

"And we get the note ourselves and get it back to Charlene's mom!" Smashie shook her head sadly. "Mrs. Stott's feelings are going to be terribly hurt," she said. "Betrayed by her own daughter!"

"I know," said Dontel soberly. "It would be like me stealing my dad's dental drill."

"Ugh," said Smashie. "I think a lot of people would be glad if you did that, actually."

"Hrmm," said Dontel.

And, their crackers eaten and milk drunk, they put their heads together and planned the dance.

The following day, all was chaos for the dress rehearsal. The two third-grade classes were in the auditorium. Ms. Early and Miss Dismont were shouting instructions, and there were some other grown-ups, family members of the performers, milling about as well, helping.

"Let's just run through all the dances!" shouted Ms. Early. She clapped her hands. "Line up and we'll go straight through." And they did. At last it was time to tweak the particulars of the Mashed Potato. Smashie and Dontel exchanged glances.

"We thought this one would look better if we danced it in two rows on the diagonals, Ms. Early," said Dontel. "With partners."

"Can we pick our partners?" Charlene asked quickly.

"Ooh, she wants to dance with Carlos," said Siggie.

"Don't tease," said John. "One day it might be you."

Charlene blushed. "You all leave me alone!"

"No," said Smashie. "We thought it would look good if we were all in height order."

"That's a great idea," said Miss Dismont. "Come on, kids, line yourselves up by height, smallest to tallest, please." And after some tussling and arguing and standing back-to-back with witnesses, the third grade was in a perfect ascending line of height.

"Rats," muttered Charlene. For she was several inches taller than Carlos. Jacinda, clocking in at the same height, was his partner. Charlene cast her an anguished look, and Jacinda looked apologetically back.

But Dontel and Smashie looked at each other with satisfaction. For Dontel matched with Charlene.

Cyrus matched with Smashie. "Boy, am I glad we're the same height," said Cyrus to Smashie. "Thank you for helping me again last night."

Smashie beamed at him. "No problem. I'm glad we're partners, too. You've really improved! We'll have a good time with this one." Then, remembering her and Dontel's plan, she told him, "Just follow my lead."

"Will do," said Cyrus.

And the Mashed Potato went off without a hitch.

Sweaty and satisfied with the third-graders' dancing as she was, Smashie couldn't help but feel a pang when the musical acts rehearsed. What would it be like to sing in front of everybody, like Tatiana was doing? Oh, well. As Smashie's mother had said, her job this time was to do her best with the role she was given and just make sure she was prepared the next time an opportunity to sing came around.

Onstage, Dontel was practicing his piece about astronomy and the night sky.

"Great job," Smashie whispered to him as he came offstage to join her.

"Thanks," said Dontel.

"We still have the brownies for Mr. Bloom, remember, for when he comes back from his conference."

"Stale," said Dontel sadly.

"Yes," said Smashie. "And we have no more time to bake fresh ones! Not if we are going to stop this crime! We will have to hope he understands the gesture."

Onstage, John sat at the piano. But he couldn't bring himself to touch the keys.

"It's okay," soothed Miss Dismont. "Just close your eyes and pretend no one is here."

"If I close my eyes I can't see the keys," said John miserably. He hung his head.

"Come with me, John," said Ms. Early, and she led him away for a heart-to-heart. The children couldn't hear what she said, but they could see John shaking his head firmly from side to side.

"I don't think he'll be able to do it," said Dontel.

"Poor guy," said Smashie sympathetically. "He's usually so fierce and brave."

"Well, we know performing can be the pits," said Dontel. "Remember that basketball game where your grammy and my dad made us dance?"

And Smashie shuddered to remember. There had been boos.

She turned to the rest of the third grade. "We can't tease him," she said, eyeing Siggie and Billy. A light died in their eyes. "We have to make him feel like he can do it." She couldn't help but feel the irony of the situation, though. Here was Smashie, wanting to sing, and there was John, not wanting to. But Smashie couldn't help but admire the way he was attacking a fear like this. She just hoped he could do it.

"If he can't," said Joyce, "let's cover for his number and pretend it was never supposed to happen."

"But then we won't dance the Mashed Potato!" cried Charlene. "That's the dance that goes with John's piece."

"Oh, we'll dance it, all right," said Dontel grimly, pegging her with a look. "We'll dance it if it's the last thing we do."

"Well, it is the last thing we do," said Joyce practically. "It's the end of the Hair Extravaganza and Musicale."

"Everybody, just hope," said Smashie. "Alonso, you and John are good friends. Can you help him?"

"I can try," said Alonso. "I can offer to do the percussion for his song so he's not all alone onstage."

"Great idea," said Dontel. "Let's hope it works."

But their worry was interrupted by Tatiana, careening into the gym.

"Look!" she cried. "LOOK! It's a jar of our missing Herr Goop!"

CHAPTER 37

Double Layers

"What?!"

"Where?!" The class was agog.

"It was on the bookcase in the reading corner!" Tatiana said breathlessly. "I went back to Room 11 to get the lyrics for my song and saw it there. Someone must have just set it down there while we were all doing our work."

"Someone?" muttered Dontel to Smashie. "Someone named Charlene, is what I think. My bet is that it's a jar she already took and used for one of the codes to Carlos."

"Dontel! I bet you're right!"

"And I bet the jar she said was from a 'mysterious benefactor' was a jar she had already used for the codes, too," said Dontel. "That's why the label was thicker on that jar—because Charlene put a clean label *over* the coded one. So it was a double layer! And then, just now, she planted this other jar in the reading corner. I bet that one has a double layer of labels, too."

Smashie agreed. "I think that's all correct," she said. "Mrs. Stott laughed when I mentioned the mysterious benefactor during my haircut. I thought she was just happy about having a mysterious benefactor with a trained monkey, but now I think—"

"Charlene," finished Dontel. "She made it all up."

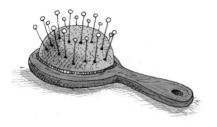

CHAPTER 38

The Third-Grade Hair Extravaganza and Musicale!

If the final rehearsal had been hectic, the night of the actual performance the next day was energized chaos. Rooms 11 and 12 were filled with students dressed in ways that fit their numbers and with family members trying to put finishing touches on their children before the teachers shooed them into the auditorium to watch the show. Charlene and her mother were racing about like mad things, twisting hair into lengthened and molded shapes for the first number, the Pony.

"Smashie," Dontel said, "this is it. This is the night we find out what's going on for real."

"I know," said Smashie. "Dontel, you be sure to dance Charlene away from Jacinda and Carlos in the Mashed Potato. I've got to be clear to grab that note!"

"I will," Dontel promised. "But keep your voice down! The place is crawling with family members!"

And sure enough, behind them were adults, addressing each other politely.

"I'm Gloria Morales," said Jacinda's mom. "And you are?"

"Manuel Garcia," said Carlos's dad. "Nice to meet you. What do you do?"

"I'm a patent lawyer," said Mrs. Morales. "And you?"

"I own a hair salon."

From the direction of Charlene and her mother came a snort. A loud one.

But Mr. Garcia and Mrs. Morales didn't seem to notice.

"I'm out of work at the moment," said Jacinda's dad. "You know how it is."

"I sure do," said another parent, and he and Jacinda's dad exchanged head shakes and sighs.

"Do you know Cynthia Hull?" Mrs. Morales asked Mr. Garcia, gesturing to Cyrus's mom. "She and her husband own Hulls' Auto Body."

"I certainly do," said Mr. Garcia, shaking Mrs. Hull's hand warmly. "She has fixed my car many times."

"I'm a phlebotomist," said Smashie's mother, who already knew all the others. She gestured to Grammy. "This is my mother, Sue."

"And I," said Grammy, "am mercifully retired. Smashie and Dontel, shouldn't you be doing a last-minute rehearsal with your first group of dancers?"

The two investigators jumped. "Yes!" they said. "Come on, Pony group!"

"We aren't done with their hair!" wailed Charlene. "There's still Billy to do!"

"I think Cyrus still needs his hair done, too, Charlene," said Dontel, picking up the jar of goop Tatiana had found, then picking discreetly at the label. But before Smashie could see if the double-label theory was correct, Mr. Garcia was talking over her head.

"Perhaps I could help," he offered.

"No, thanks," said Charlene. "We've got it." But Charlene looked worried as she took the jar from Dontel and began to style the hair of a surprised Cyrus from behind. And when she was done, the pony she created on his head was as magnificent as it had been the other day.

Meanwhile, Billy Kamarski was talking to his mother behind them. "It's a set of roller-skate wheels, Mom!" he was saying. "And they're permanent!"

"PERMANENT? Billy Kamarski—"

"Yep," said Billy cheerfully. "You'll just have to get used to having a set of roller-skate wheels for a son."

"All parents except the designated helpers should head to the auditorium, please!" called Ms. Early. "Our show is going to start in just five minutes."

There was a rush for the door, with cries of "Break a leg!" and "Head up, John! We're proud of you!" and "A SET OF ROLLER-SKATE WHEELS?!" from the adults as they left the room.

The scent of lavender was overpowering, but the Pony children looked fantastic. They were ready.

Mrs. Armstrong stood at the apron of the stage. "I would like to take this opportunity to welcome our third-grade families and friends to the Room 11 and Room 12 Hair Extravaganza and Musicale." Mrs. Armstrong cast an eye at the children in the wings. "And I'd like to thank the students for their hard work and their choice of . . . appropriate material. I was quite worried for a moment. Ill, even. But we worked through those kinks, so now, without further ado, here are Ms. Early and Miss Dismont, our third-grade teachers."

Ms. Early and Miss Dismont swept onto the stage to join her. And, surprise of surprises, their hair was done in shapes as well! Ms. Early's was in the shape of a dancing shoe, to represent the dancing part of the evening, and Miss Dismont's loaf of hair was molded into a treble clef, to represent the musical numbers. They looked magnificent, and the audience and third-graders went wild.

"Good evening!" Ms. Early cried as the noise died down. "Tonight we will be hearing songs, some older and some newer, and in between each, you will see some marvelous sixties go-go dancing! Special thanks to Sue Tango and Dr. Martin Marquise for helping our student choreographers, Smashie McPerter and Dontel Marquise, create the dance numbers. And special thanks to Charlene Stott and her mother, Betty Stott, for all their work on the children's hairstyles as well."

The audience cheered and clapped. Only a few people heard the plaintive cry of Billy Kamarski's mother.

"We are so pleased to see so many families and staff members of the Rebecca Lee Crumpler Elementary School here to support our students," Miss Dismont added. "I'd also like to extend a special thank-you to Mr. Bloom, Miss Martone, and Mr. Flange, all of whom have been great friends to Rooms 11 and 12 during this process. Thank you for coming tonight."

Smashie gulped. So Mr. Bloom *was* here in the audience. She hoped he would stay long enough for her to give him the apology brownies that she had brought backstage from her cubby, stale as they were. *Maybe our dances will win him back over,* she thought, and vowed to do her very best. *After all, he said he was a fan of sixties go-go dancing.*

"So let's start the show!" said Miss Dismont. "MUSIC!" she shouted offstage, and Walter from Room 12 pressed PLAY on the sound system.

The music for the Pony started, and the class Ponied across the stage just as Smashie and Dontel had taught them, arms swinging, feet shifting. "Energy!" shouted Smashie under the cover of the music, and the children picked it up even more, finally Ponying with perfect hoofwork off the stage. The audience went wild.

"Smashie, that was great!" cried Mrs. Stott from the wings.

"Thanks," said Smashie modestly. Cyrus hugged her.

"Thank you for helping me," he said. "I felt like I was really dancing that time!"

"You looked it, too," said Smashie. "I'm proud as heck of you!"

But there was no time for more, for the next act

was already up. Siggie was onstage with a table full of objects — an apple, a shoe, a stapler, an orange, and about ten other things.

"Tonight," he said, "I am going to perform a feat of alphabetization. I will put all of these objects — which I have never seen before now — in alphabetical order by the time my backup singers" — he nodded toward the children ranged behind him, hair done up into sculptures of letters — "can sing the alphabet in English. And then, while they sing the alphabet in Spanish, I'll alphabetize the same objects but using their Spanish names!"

"Whoo!" called some parents. "Let's see it!"

"A, B, C, D, E, F, G," sang the children as Siggie's hands moved like lightning to order the objects. He didn't even hesitate to put the shoe before the stapler, and before the singers reached Z, he was done.

"Anchovies, apple, beetle, blender, cheese . . ." he began. The audience applauded when he reached the end, but Siggie held up his hand and the singers began to sing the alphabet in Spanish. Once again, Siggie was done realphabetizing the objects before the singers had finished the song.

"*Anchoas, escarabajo, grapadora, licuadora...*" Siggie went through them all, and once again, he'd made not a single error.

"What skill!" cried Mr. Garcia from the audience.

"You know it!" said Mrs. Higgins from the crowd.

But there was no time for Smashie and Dontel to congratulate Siggie when he came offstage, as they were already organizing the other children to dance the Swim. The dance went beautifully, and before they knew it, Alonso, his hair in the shape of an infinity sign to represent the "Endless" part of the "Endless Amour" song, was already dueting with Lilia, whose hair was molded into a heart to represent the "Amour" part. The backup dancers looked fabulous as well, with their hair in smaller musical notes, infinity signs, and hearts.

"It's all going so quickly!" said John, who looked almost sick with stage fright. But he was right. It was almost time for the Temptation Walk.

"Smashie." Dontel grabbed her by the elbow. "Look at Charlene's left sock. But be discreet about it!"

Smashie looked casually around, but she couldn't help but startle at the sight of a paper peeping over

the edge of Charlene's striped sock above her go-go boot. The Mashed Potato might be the only dance Charlene was to perform, given that her hair duties were keeping her busy, but it was clear that she was ready to go on with her nefarious plan to betray her own mother. Smashie looked at Dontel and nodded.

The Temptation Walk began with high energy, and the children moved perfectly in its squares and diagonals around the stage.

And then Dontel was onstage, about to speak his astronomy piece. "I'd like to dedicate this piece to Mr. Bloom," said Dontel, "who has always been a wonderful mentor to me about space."

"Wahoo!" called Mr. Bloom as the adults cheered, and Smashie's heart leaped within her. Maybe his UFO conference had put him in a forgiving frame of mind.

"The stars we see at night look like pricks of light, but are they?" Dontel asked the audience. "No. They are balls of fire. They are galaxies swirling and colliding as they move through space. . . ."

As soon as Dontel was done with his piece, there was Smashie, leading the Shimmy in her most astronomy-like way right behind him. Dontel joined in with the dancers, and, finally, offstage they went, to more applause and cheers.

"We can't change hair this fast," panted Charlene. "Everybody has a different shape for each dance! Alonso has to turn from an infinity sign into something to do with Hyacinth Rooney now! Mom, what can we do?"

"I could help," said Carlos shyly. "I've watched you do it, and I bet I could do a good job."

"NO NEED!" shouted Smashie. The last thing she and Dontel wanted was a new way for Charlene and Carlos to get in contact before the Mashed Potato, for heaven's sake.

"We need Carlos to . . . to help Cyrus," said Dontel, thinking quickly. "Can you help him with the steps for the next number?"

"Could you?" asked Cyrus eagerly. "I am a little dicey on the Mashed Potato still."

"I sure can," said Carlos. He glanced over at Charlene. "It's . . . it's my favorite one."

"We'll be fine, Charlene," said Mrs. Stott soothingly.

She was working on the heads for Tatiana's number, and they were magnificent.

Dontel and Smashie looked at each other, limp with relief. But not for long. After Tatiana's wonderful skating number and the Skate dance, there was John, being led onto the stage by Ms. Early. They watched him take in a deep breath as Alonso, with a drum and a brush, got ready to percuss.

There was a pause. Then a longer pause.

The audience waited.

John closed his eyes. He opened them. Alonso gave an encouraging nod. And then, wonder of wonders, John's fingers hit the keys and he began to sing.

"Come on over to my place!
If you can, well, in that case,
I'll give you some casserole and some cake, too—hey!
Come on over to my place!
I'll give you shish kebab and some steak, too—hey!"

The audience whistled and cheered. John was a changed boy, confident at his piano. Alonso moved his head in time with the music, and the auditorium was filled with applause and cries.

And then it was over.

"I am so proud of you!"

"Me too, man!"

"You killed it!"

"And your neck looked great!"

Smashie and Dontel were proud of John, too, but their stomachs were full of butterflies. For now was the time.

"Smashie," said Dontel, "we're about to do the Mashed Potato."

"I know." Smashie gulped.

"Everything depends on this dance," whispered Dontel. "We can't mess it up! We have to save Charlene's mother from Charlene letting Carlos steal the hair goop formula!"

And, with hair in the shapes of potatoes, bowls, and mashers, the dancers lined up by height with their partners and got ready for the Mashed Potato.

Dontel looked at the paired children. His jaw dropped.

"Of course," he said. "Smashie!"

"Yes?" said Smashie.

"My goodness! Do you see it, too?"

"Well, yes," said Smashie. Hadn't she seen that paper peeping out of Charlene's sock ages ago? "Duh."

Dontel looked at her hard. "And you understand what we have to do now?" he said urgently.

"You bet I do," said Smashie. What did he take her for? The goal had been clear since yesterday. "Let's get on it!"

And out onto the stage they danced.

CHAPTER 39

A Mess of a Dance

"And now for our finale!" cried Miss Dismont. "THE MASHED POTATO!"

Heart pounding, out danced Smashie right beside Cyrus at the back of the stage. At this moment, Smashie knew her go-go-dancing costume was every bit as much an Investigator Suit as her red jacket and tool belt had been. She looked across the stage at Dontel and Charlene in the opposite back corner. Carlos and Jacinda were ready in the corner opposite Smashie and Cyrus at the front. And then it started. Heels twisting, arms mashing, the group began to wiggle and dance in the directions Smashie and Dontel had taught them. And then Smashie saw. Charlene—the piece of paper still sticking up from her go-go boot—was determinedly trying to lead Dontel in the direction of Carlos.

"Come on, Cyrus." Smashie puffed under the cover of the music. "We're switching things up a bit. Follow me!"

"That's what I'm doing anyway." Cyrus huffed and danced with her across the midpoint of the stage. Little did he know that they were blocking Charlene from her nefarious intentions to betray her mother for the sake of like-like!

But what was this? Dontel appeared in front of Smashie, Mashed Potatoing hard in her direction. He was forcing her away from Charlene.

Cyrus stumbled.

"What are you doing?" Smashie hissed to Dontel.

"What are *you* doing?" he hissed back.

The dance was growing chaotic. With Smashie and Dontel in the wrong places, nobody knew where to go. So they Mashed Potatoed in place, with Charlene the only one moving purposefully across the stage. Toward Carlos.

And Dontel was doing nothing to stop her.

I won't have it, thought Smashie resolutely, and, her hair potato quivering on the top of her head, she Mashed Potatoed Cyrus once more across the stage to intercept her classmate.

But again Dontel cut her off.

Smashie forced him to dance backward away from her.

Dontel retaliated by dancing her forward toward the wings.

On and on they tussled, each moving the other back and forth, with no real progress made, as Charlene got ever closer to Carlos.

"Why are you messing everything up?" Dontel whisper-shouted to Smashie.

"I'm trying to do what's right!" said Smashie.

"Well, so am I!" And the two were locked in dance battle as, behind them, Charlene reached her goal. One more heel twist and she was in front of Carlos and Jacinda.

And a hand reached down into Charlene's boot and extracted the paper.

"Got it!"

But it wasn't Carlos who was speaking in triumph. It was Jacinda.

The dancing came to a screeching halt.

"What's happening?"

"Why are we stopping?"

"What is Jacinda doing?"

"Why did Smashie and Dontel change up the dance?"

Everyone was confused. In the audience, the

parents whispered and exchanged puzzled looks. In the wings, Ms. Early and Miss Dismont looked shocked.

Dontel and Smashie locked eyes. "Dontel!" she cried. "What's going on?"

"This," said Dontel, and, crossing over to Jacinda, he took the paper from her startled hand, leaped into the audience, and handed it to Mrs. Morales, Jacinda's mother. "I believe you'll need it," he said.

All chaos broke loose.

CHAPTER 40

Revelations

Charlene was sobbing. Jacinda was indignant. Mrs. Morales was puzzled, and nobody knew what was happening. Everybody was trying to make sense of the non-end of the show.

Ms. Early stood onstage and clapped her hands. "Dontel Marquise," she called. "And, if I know anything, Smashie McPerter. Come up here. I think you two have some explaining to do."

Smashie threw up her hands. "What do I know?

Dontel, why did you give that paper to Jacinda's mom?"

"Yes," said Mrs. Morales, puzzled. "Why? What is it?"

"It goes with these." Jacinda crossed over to her mother and handed her three other pieces of paper. "We'll need them all."

"Jacinda!"

"Dontel!"

"Charlene!"

Everyone was yelling at everybody else, and nobody could make head or tail of a thing. The adults were concerned, and the rest of the third-graders were unsure whether or not to leave their Mashed Potato positions.

"BY THUNDER, WHAT IS GOING ON HERE?" It was Mr. Bloom. "Nobody knows what in tarnation you are talking about, Mr. M. and Miss McP.!"

"Yes!" cried Mrs. Armstrong. "You are making me ILL with worry!"

"Begin at the beginning, Dontel and Smashie," said Ms. Early. "And don't stop until we all understand why our musicale had to be disrupted."

"It had better be good," said Siggie.

"Everybody better come up on the stage," said Smashie. "It's kind of a long story. And I don't even get the end of it myself. "

So the families clumped up the stage stairs and joined their children. Miss Dismont began to pass around the plates of refreshments Cyrus had made as Dontel started the tale.

"It all started with the missing jars of Herr Goop," Dontel began. "You all remember how we worried they were being stolen, Room 11?"

Room 11, scattered around the stage, nodded. Family members leaned toward their children, and whispered explanations filled the air.

"Well, it turns out we were right. They *were* taken."

"Are you accusing Mr. Bloom *again?*" Tatiana was outraged.

"What?!" cried Mrs. Armstrong. "Please do not tell me you are accusing a treasured member of our staff! Why, I will be SO ILL I'LL NEED A NIGHT NURSE! I'll—"

"No!" said Smashie hastily. "We thought it was

him once, but we were wrong! He only found the first jar!"

"We keep trying to tell him we're sorry — we even baked him some apology brownies a few days ago, but they are yucky now," said Dontel.

"You poor kids," said Mr. Bloom. "Why, I forgave you ages ago. Just away at my UFO convention and no way of telling ya. No need for apology brownies. I know how it is to be eight years old and get carried away. Why, one time, I was convinced my own mother took my toy helicopter. Why would the woman want it? I don't know. But it made all kinds of sense to me at the time." He shook his head and patted their shoulders. "You're my little friends. Of course I forgive you."

Smashie's eyes filled. She was very sorry, and very grateful. Smashie's mother and Grammy hugged her shoulders.

"Back to the mystery, Smashie and Dontel," said Joyce firmly.

"We figured it was too much of a coincidence for the next two jars to go missing," said Smashie. "So we knew something was afoot, even if we didn't know what."

"I thought something was afoot after the first jar, too," cried Charlene. "When that jar was gone, I was sure Carlos had taken it to give to his father so Mr. Garcia could figure out what was in our Herr Goop and make it and sell it as his own!"

"What!" cried Carlos and Mr. Garcia at the same time.

"Oh!" said Joyce. "So that's why you were staring at him during that tag game."

Charlene nodded. Carlos looked crestfallen.

"Please," said Mr. Garcia, startled. "What are you talking about?"

"You know what she's talking about!" cried Mrs. Stott. "I overheard you telling the other gals at the salon that you didn't believe I made our goop in my own kitchen. You said I had to have made it in your salon, using your ingredients, and therefore it might as well have your name on it!"

Mr. Garcia looked puzzled. Then his face cleared. "Mrs. Stott," he said, "you misunderstood. I was talking about the birthday cake one of the stylists made and served at our salon party for my wife. I was being rude about the stylist's cooking, for which I am sorry, but I never, ever meant your goop. Why, you invented that goop and it's genius!"

Mrs. Stott's jaw dropped.

"Is this why you left my salon?" Mr. Garcia asked her.

"Yes," said Mrs. Stott. "It is."

"Please come back," pleaded Mr. Garcia. "The salon hasn't been the same without your creativity. And your real gift is sculpture. We need you!"

Charlene's mother blushed, and her shoulders sagged with relief. "Mr. Garcia, thank you! I'd love to come back. I miss your salon, and it really has not been all that much fun trying to strike out on my own."

"Back to the mystery, please," said John. "I mean, I'm glad for you and all, Mrs. Stott, but I still don't get what's going on."

"We didn't either, at first," said Smashie. "We thought the goop was just being stolen."

"I helped people think that," confessed Charlene. "I shouted when the second one disappeared so no one would suspect *me* of stealing our own goop. But then Dontel must have seen one of the missing jars in the gym—"

"And it had a secret code on it!" Dontel finished.

There were many gasps.

"A secret code?"

"What was it?"

Smashie and Dontel explained the math they had used to figure it out.

"Yes," said Charlene. "That was it."

"Well, I'm glad, at least, you were paying attention in math class," said Ms. Early. "Please go on, Smashie and Dontel."

"We figured out pretty quickly it must have been Charlene who was writing the codes and taking the jars to hide in the gym for someone else to find," said Dontel.

"Dontel was the one who figured that out," said Smashie.

"But why was she doing that? What did the codes lead to?" asked a parent.

"Messages," said Dontel. "All over town. At first we thought that they were just, uh—notes," said Dontel delicately. "To Carlos."

Smashie was less delicate. "Because of all the silly like-like talk."

"You thought I was sending Carlos like-like notes? Sheesh!" Charlene was very put out.

Carlos cast his eyes down sadly.

"Yes," said Smashie. "But then when I got my hair cut—"

"You got your hair cut?" asked Miss Dismont. "Why, it looks just the same."

"So they tell me," said Smashie flatly. "Anyway, when I got my hair cut by Mrs. Stott, Charlene had put a last, nearly whole jar that Mrs. Stott had scraped together from the last of her ingredients into a bag. I knew that it just had to have a code on it. And I was right—it did! So when Mrs. Stott gave me the bag to bring to school, it meant that Dontel and I got to the secret message before Charlene's partner in crime did."

"I was so mad my mom gave you that jar," admitted Charlene. "I was terrified I wouldn't be able to hide it in the gym!"

"I bet," said Smashie. "Anyway, when we found the message, it wasn't a regular old like-like note at all! It turned out to be a part of the Herr Goop recipe!"

"Charlene!" cried Mrs. Stott. "Were you giving our recipe away to Carlos because *you* thought his dad had the rights to it?"

"No!" cried Charlene. "Mom, how could you even think that?"

"We thought that, too," confessed Dontel. "But we were wrong. We knew Charlene was writing the codes and taking the jars and leaving them to be found, but it turned out it had nothing to do with Carlos. And everything to do with you, Mrs. Stott."

"What do you mean?" asked Mrs. Stott. "And, Charlene, if you took all the jars meant for your class—"

"Except the first one." Smashie interrupted.

"—and used them for this"—Mrs. Stott fought for the words—"code thing, how come we still had them all for tonight?"

"When I took the second one back, I pretended you had replaced one of the jars and brought it to school for us," said Charlene, her eyes welling up a bit with the admission of her fib. "I pretended you had a mysterious benefactor."

"Oh!" said Mrs. Stott. "So you weren't just kidding around when you mentioned a mysterious benefactor, Smashie."

"Nope," said Smashie. "I still thought that was true at that point."

"And I put the last missing jar back in the reading corner so someone in our own class would find it and think I'd just been careless," Charlene confessed.

"I'm the one who found it," said Tatiana.

"What I don't get," said Siggie, "is how you managed to take the jars out from under our very noses. With the exception of the one that rolled away, the others were taken when we were all there in Room 11."

"Well"—Charlene's voice was teary—"it was pretty easy. You people don't zip your backpacks much. Mom, I'm so sorry!" Charlene's eyes filled again. "I was lying and pretending all over the place!"

Smashie was full of sympathy. She had been just as conflicted about fibbing as Charlene. *On the other side of the coin, though,* she thought, *I was fibbing for justice.* But who could say where the line for fibbing was drawn? Smashie shook her head.

"Charlene did pretend," said Dontel. "When I peeled up the label on the jar before our last dance tonight, I saw one of the old codes underneath. So it just confirmed to me that Charlene had taken the other, coded jars and then arranged to have them reappear with new, code-less labels on the top."

"Yes," said Smashie. "But now you have lost even me. I thought we had figured out that Carlos was going to get the last part of the formula during the Mashed Potato, and that it was my job to take it from Charlene and make sure he didn't get it. How did you figure out that Jacinda was Charlene's real partner in crime?"

"It was when we all lined up in height order tonight," said Dontel. "I realized then that in a black sneaky Thief Suit, like the one we saw at the Dairy Delight, Jacinda is the same height as Carlos and would look the same. They are both excellent runners, too. And I knew how worried Charlene was about her mom's business, and I remembered that Mrs. Morales was a patent lawyer, and it all . . . it all just fell into place. I knew Charlene was just trying to get the goop patented in her mom's name before someone else did it first!"

"You've got it exactly," said Charlene, her eyes filling with tears again. "Even though you told us that Mr. Bloom had the first jar, I couldn't shake the worry that Carlos was trying to get my mom's goop. He kept staring at me!"

"Charlene—" said Joyce gently. But Smashie interrupted.

"Dontel, I had no idea!" cried Smashie. "I thought you had gone nuts and wanted Carlos's dad to have the formula after all!"

"I'm sorry, Smashie! I asked you if you understood before the dance started, and you said yes."

"I meant I understood the plan we had made," said Smashie. "Not that you had made a new one. No wonder we were dancing at cross purposes the whole time during the Mashed Potato! Our minds were not as one!"

Charlene was sobbing again. "Mom, I would never betray you! Me and Jacinda did it all for you! I wanted you to strike it rich with the goop!"

"I am more than happy to help with the patent," said Mrs. Morales.

"Why, thank you!" said Mrs. Stott.

"But why didn't you just *give* me the formula, Charlene?" asked Mrs. Morales, puzzled. "Why all the codes and running around?"

"I needed to make sure that the whole formula was never in one place, in case someone did steal it," Charlene explained. "This was important! It was top secret! It was *industrial espionage*! I couldn't trust it to a plain old piece of paper delivered all at once in just a regular old way."

Industrial espionage! Smashie couldn't wait to

add that to her and Dontel's Investigator Language list.

"So Jacinda and I devised this plan," Charlene continued.

"That first day on the blacktop?" asked Dontel.

"Yep," said Charlene.

"We all thought you were just like-liking Carlos," said Cyrus.

Charlene blushed. So did Carlos. "Well," said Charlene, "I do think he's a wonderful dancer."

"And I—I . . ." stammered Carlos, "think you are amazing at hair."

"Thank you," said Charlene, and smiled a very small, shy smile at Carlos.

"Hoo-boy," said John. "And so it begins."

"Smashie and Dontel," said Jacinda, "I'm sorry I let everyone be so mean to you about Mr. Bloom while you were investigating. I just had to throw people off the trail!"

"Yes," said Charlene. "Me too. I really apologize! I stirred the pot about Mr. Bloom and you being awful that day in the gym just because you were by the basketball bins and I needed the area clear so Jacinda could find the goop I hid!"

"It's okay," said Smashie. "We understand now that you were trying to help your mom."

"Jacinda, how did you get so involved in this?" asked her mother.

"I felt bad for Charlene and Mrs. Stott. It's hard to be out of work," said Jacinda, her lip quivering. "Daddy got laid off and he still . . ." She gulped and stopped. Her parents both put their arms around her.

"Well, it certainly is a fine goop," said Ms. Early. "I am quite enjoying my own hair sculpture!"

"I sure enjoyed mine, too," said Mr. Bloom. "But I got tired of all that extra hair and washed it out. I'm my old self again!"

Mr. Flange silently extended the near-empty jar of goop that he and Mr. Bloom had used to Charlene's mother.

But Mrs. Stott shook her head. "You keep it," she said. "We wound up with enough Herr Goop for the musicale after all, and I think it's nice for you two to have the option of lengthening and molding your hair again someday if you want to." She beamed at them. Mr. Bloom beamed back. It was hard to tell about Mr. Flange because of the size and length of his Herr Gooped mustache, but his eyes looked like they were smiling.

But not everyone was feeling the moment. "This goop stuff washes OUT?" Mrs. Kamarski exclaimed. "Billy Kamarski, why would you tell me it was permanent?"

"Um, because it was funny?"

"We'll see how funny it is when I get you home with your hair washed in the tub!"

"Aw, Mom!"

"I'm not tired of my old self," said Smashie unhappily. "I liked my old hair self. Now my hair goes in a lot of different directions when I don't have the goop in."

"I am more than happy to . . . recut anyone's hair," said Mr. Garcia. "For free, to celebrate Mrs. Stott's return to my salon."

"Thank you!" cried Joyce.

"Yes, thank you," said Smashie, fully aware that nobody thought she needed a new cut.

"I look forward to making your hair beautiful," Mr. Garcia said to Joyce, and Joyce and he exchanged beams.

"Smashie and Dontel," said Ms. Early, "I would like to applaud your thinking, even if it has been a very disruptive week."

"I second that!" said Miss Dismont. "And anyone using math to solve a mystery is an A-plus in my book! Now I think we should celebrate the whole third grade and this Hair Extravaganza and Musicale and its wonderful ending," she continued. "Let's have a party!"

"A dance party!" cried Jacinda.

"Yay! Yes!" cried the children.

"I know a great dance!" cried Mr. Bloom. "In keeping with the sixties stuff! It's called the Jerk!"

And before Mrs. Armstrong could say a word of protest or about being ill, Mr. Bloom had the sound system blaring the Larks, and all the adults were moving.

"Woo-hoo!" cried the dancers.

"Whee!" cried the teachers.

And even Mrs. Armstrong moved her arms in the

appropriate motions for the Jerk. Twice, even, she was seen to smile.

The music ended, and Ms. Early went up to the stage and took the microphone.

"I have another fun idea," she said to the audience. "Dontel and his dad and Smashie's grammy can teach everyone another sixties dance. It's called the Loco-Motion."

"What about me?" cried Smashie, stung. "Can't I help teach it, too?"

"No," said Ms. Early. "Because we need you to sing the song while we dance."

"Sing . . . sing the song?" said Smashie, hardly daring to hope.

"Yes!" cried the audience as a whole.

Smashie caught her mother's eye.

"Opportunity," said her mother.

"And I know just what to sing," said Smashie.

"I'll improv the piano for you!" said John.

Smashie blinked with joy. "Thank you, Ms. Early!" She hugged her teacher. Ms. Early hugged her back. Then Smashie leaped to the front of the stage, feeling as light as air. While everybody lined up behind

Dontel and Dr. Marquise and Grammy to learn the dance, she took up the microphone. "These aren't going to be the real lyrics to 'The Loco-Motion,'" she said. "I'm going to make some up in honor of Ms. Early and her tips about thinking. Me and Dontel couldn't have solved this mystery without them."

And then, to the tune of "The Loco-Motion," Smashie began to sing as loudly as she could.

"Everybody needs to think and come and dance now!
Come on, third grade, motion sparks the notion!
You've got to use your brains if you want to advance now!
Come on, third grade, motion sparks the notion!"

Smashie was loud but the audience was louder. Everybody sang and danced, and nothing had ever felt quite so wonderful.